THE RIGHT MEMBERS CLUB

LOUIS URBANOWSKI

SHILKA PUBLISHING

THE GREASY POLE

*Breaking News: Belinda Blows It! Who is Jackson Pierce?
As the newly elected leader of the Labour Party promises change and
surges in the polls, we learn more about him — click here for his
biography*

1

f the British public learned the truth, they'd laugh.

The starting pistol on the general election, or as it would later be known, 'The Last General Election', had been fired.

The Right Members Club were not spies. There was no need for disguises or gadgets or licences to kill. Hell, William Purcell could walk right up to someone and explain who he was and what he did and all he'd get would be a slap on the shoulder and a laugh.

As the opening notes of *Question Time* tinkled from the old TV on wheels, William and his Members waited for a specific answer. Inducted at their lowest, only the most pathetic of the downtrodden get into his club: disgraced MPs, forgotten ministers, nameless faceless politicians discarded on the scrapheap, all flung so far from the backbenches they couldn't remember how deceptively uncomfortable they'd been.

William understood the system perfectly. The people elected the government; the government ran the country. Unfortunately, this arrangement frequently ended in tears. Fingers got pointed and blame assigned. Not to be deterred, the electorate would dust themselves down and simply try again, sometimes in anger, sometimes in the foolish hope that the next time they'd get it right.

But William was a man with a job, and that job was pruning. A bad apple here, an errant branch of rhetoric there. If Britain was to endure, then it needed plain sailing through calm waters. As far as William was concerned, the people elected the government, the government ran the country and the Right Members Club made sure it all stayed exceedingly boring.

The Club let the front line of politics frolic, there in the shadows as a safety net for when those in the spotlight inevitably discovered that sticking their fingers into the nation's plug sockets was a bad idea.

William settled into his high-back chair, letting the stiff leather squeak beneath him. The unmistakable tang of stale beer and varnished wood was oddly comforting. This was the ideal setting from which to conduct politics. The Club's head-quarters, the Omnibar, operated in plain sight behind the boarded-up windows of just another failed pub. He sipped his bitter and let out a breath of relaxation, of focus. It was the culmination of their hard work on their most recent pruning job: Belinda Carmichael.

'Billy the teleprompter cost a grand and a rather nice Macallan in the end. Shall I take it out of the tin?' Zachary asked over by the bar.

'Mmm.' William waved a hand, focusing on the TV.

'Does he call himself that, Billy the teleprompter?' Susie asked.

'Only when he's prompting, probably.' Zachary said, distracted as he rattled the lid off the petty cash.

This general election was different. Britain wasn't happy. Blame was everywhere and indiscriminate. Small boats floated on the sea of public consciousness. The existing Conservative government had been in place for over a decade but was now crumbling. It was death by a thousand cuts: scandals piled high, services cut and a cost-of-living crisis delivering despair to households more efficiently than the Post Office ever could.

A fertile soil, ready for sowing. One that had allowed the nationalistic Belinda Carmichael and her Mend party to sprout.

Only instead of 'Make-do and mend' she had coined 'Make-new and mend'. She deserved to go for that horrid wordplay alone in truth. With rumours of funding from hedge fund types across the pond verified, William considered her a monster truck in a car park of Morris Minors. Her platform would only serve to destabilise Britain and caricature it as the ironic island that hated foreigners.

The Right Members Club thought long and hard before intervening. William saw them as tools—of consistency. Weapons—of reason. Carmichael was to be the latest excision; her downfall would allow the election to breathe. *This isn't about left or right, this is about morons that need taking down a peg or two.*

Katie Turner, the host, walked out to the applause of the *Question Time* audience. Each of the leaders would have an *intimate* (a funny way to put it, William thought) session. Pre-vetted questions with polished answers, no doubt. Belinda Carmichael was up first; the BBC wanted to start with a bang.

Instead, she stood at the lectern with almost a whimper. It was part of her appeal. Unassuming and plain. It lulled people in. She could be a mum, an aunt or the sweet lady down the street whose grass sometimes needed cutting. That she had whole streets of properties in an investment portfolio was strangely absent from the manifesto. But when she spoke, the fire came. And it could burn.

Jessica and Susie took seats next to William.

'And the auto-cue will be wiped?' Susie asked.

'It's a brand name—*Autocue*—a British company. Maybe Belinda will appreciate that,' Zachary said.

'It best be wiped. Remember that trouble with the Foreign Office?' Jessica laughed.

'Zachary has assured me. It will flash, she'll say it, and then it will be as if it was never there.'

Katie Turner introduced Carmichael and then turned to the audience for the first question.

It came from a middle-aged white man, because of course it did, and was dispatched with consummate professionalism. In fact, the first couple of questions were nothing more than dangling morsels snaffled by the precision of Belinda's bite.

The existing government hadn't built enough homes, protected wages or clamped down on the profiteering of energy firms. Border police were ceremonial statues overseeing the silent invasion of this once-great isle. Sound-bite heavy, beautifully canned answers that painted her as future leader.

Derek wandered over, Horace too. 'She's doing well,' the first said.

'Maybe she'll breeze past it,' the second added.

'Focus. Patience. Adaptation,' William offered the group, aware his words sounded dangerously like political slogans or teams on *The Apprentice*.

The next question came from a young man. He stuttered in the run-up, which served to focus all onto his words.

'What do you say to—to—to those who say you and your party are racist?'

William could feel the other pairs of eyes looking at him. He kept his gaze squarely on the television. It crackled and fizzed as if it could feel the stakes.

Belinda welcomed the question, her arms dropping to her side, shoulders relaxed. She took a breath, smiled and answered: 'We are racist, yes.'

For a moment it felt like the television would draw all oxygen into it. The collective intake of breath in the studio was staggering. Katie Turner, the host, famous for being unflappable—*flapped.*

Belinda heard herself. Her lips pursed in and out as if chewing over the four words. Her arms came up again and gripped the lectern. William noticed her knuckles whitening, such was the grip.

'I misspoke. We are racist, yes. No. Fuck. Not fuck. Sorry. The auto-cue . . . can we cut to break?'

Katie Turner was back in control. No doubt the producers were screaming blue murder in her ear.

'Ms Carmichael, we are live, and as we've already explained, the auto-cue is switched off. I must remind you, please do not swear. Can I confirm what you said, that you are indeed racist?'

'It was on. It said "fuck, I'm racist". Fuck!'

Bedlam met Belinda. She didn't have time to speak again before the booing started. A cup full of beer, at least William hoped it was beer, showered her. And then another, and then a pork pie and some chips. The audience had transformed into a riotous gourmet zoo.

The last shot of Belinda was of her slinking off, shoulders low now, to scream and shout; at her handlers, her spin doctor, anyone and everyone who would listen.

'Well, the country heard that. Loud and clear,' William said.

Jessica leaned across. 'Spectacular. Make-do with that, Belinda. How did you know it would work?'

'Neuro-linguistic programming isn't like it's portrayed on television. It doesn't create sentiment; it only reveals it. The auto-cue, our *random* meetings in coffee houses around West-minster, all the fertiliser needed to guarantee germination, as it were.'

'Are we done, then? For this cycle, I mean. The Right Members Club have cleared the way and the electorate can get on with it, voting some poor sap into the impossible job,' Derek asked.

'I think so. Regular programming has been resumed.'

The others stood. Zachary and Susie poured another drink at the bar while Horace and Derek got chatting. It was just

Jessica, his second-in-command, who remained, and she put a hand on William's to draw him back to the screen.

'Look, they've pulled the feed. I bet the others refused to go on. Can't blame them, following that nightmare. Who was next, anyway?'

'The new guy that fronts Labour. Jackson Pierce. He'll have to launch himself another day.' William slapped his thighs and stood.

'All this fresh blood. Wonder if he'll be much of anything,' Jessica said, half interested at that point.

'Time will tell.'

And how right he was.

2

'*N*ow time for a party political broadcast from Jackson Pierce.'

Britain is dying.
No, Britain is being murdered.
Choked. Suffocated.
Left to rot by the political elite.
Eyed up by racists and bigots.
I'm going to fix her. **We're** *going to fix her.*

Vote to rise. Vote to break. Vote to shatter.

You don't care about the details. You want action.
To be safer, paid more, work less.
It's not complicated.
Admit the truth. We need to start again.

I'm Jackson Pierce, and this is my promise:
I am going to win this election and save Britain.

. . .

It was a balmy Friday evening in March. Mark Fallow finished his pint as the pub fell silent. That was all it had taken. Less than a minute of this charming man, this Jackson Pierce, to shift the political conversation in Britain and change the direction of Mark's life.

Voices erupted amongst the drinking, like bullets ricocheting off the dour fittings.

'He's insane. Who the fuck was that?'

'He's right, though, spot bollock on everything.'

'Easy to just say everything is shit.'

'But he's fit. Right, I'm registering to vote.'

Nature abhors a vacuum, so Jackson Pierce's rush to fill the void left by Carmichael's implosion seemed natural to many who followed proceedings. Overnight Jackson Pierce was a household name. Cultivating a cabal further left of the Labour Party expertly, he was quick and direct in strategy, much like his candour on television.

Other than the fact he now led Labour, little else was known about Jackson Pierce; his freshness was intoxicating. An orphan from somewhere up north with no baggage, no blunders and no bullshit.

It wasn't that, though, truly, which gave Jackson the push he needed to seize the public's attention. It was the video of Esther Murphy that had appeared two months before.

No one knew where the footage came from. A little over two minutes long, it showed the eighty-nine-year-old widow, the great-grandmother of three from rural Gloucestershire, alone at home. Slack in her threadbare chair, condensation on the windows starting to frost over. She was gaunt; the lights were dim. If Hell were a place on earth, this would be next door.

The clip culminated with an indistinct voice asking her where her fuel credit was. Why wasn't she eating? What was happening?

You had to turn up the volume to hear her ghost-like rattle. 'I don't understand. I'm cold. I'm scared.'

Esther Murphy was found dead at home the next day. People were furious. Of course, most had zero intention of doing anything about it. There were posts on social media, gossip over coffee at work, but before long there was something else to get stuck into.

Not for Mark, though. It rekindled a flame within, long thought dead, a desire to make a change. The next morning, he picked up the phone and prepared his application. He wanted to be a part of *Pierce's Promise*.

It was glamorous, valorous and other words ending in rous that Mark couldn't quite think of. His wife, the love of his life, Lucy, made a fair argument; perhaps a few beers on an empty stomach had influenced him. Mark was prone to getting carried away, he'd be the first to admit it.

Lucy spoke reason. Caution. Sense.

'Sleep on it, my love.'

Which Mark did. And he awoke the next morning to a studious Lucy in bed with the laptop.

'Look at this one—faked his own death.' She jabbed a finger at the laptop and swivelled it round.

She draped a hand over Mark's head like a shit hat, waiting for him to wake up properly.

Mark blinked as the first beams of sunlight battled the bedroom blinds.

'What on earth are you doing?'

'So, this Stonehouse guy folded his clothes up neatly on the beach and just disappeared into the ocean.'

'Right.' Mark sat up now. 'Makes sense. Who is he? Why do you care? And what's going on?'

'If you're going to do this—if we're going to do this—I want to be prepared. You saw that Carmichael torpedo herself. It doesn't take much to cock it up.'

She pushed the laptop to the side; turning to face Mark, she smiled at him in that way she did. It made him feel light, loved.

'I've not seen you as energised by something in a long time. Let's go for it. Mark Fallow, Member of Parliament. It has a nice ring to it, right?'

Lucy thought herself plain, unremarkable, forever brushing off compliments with a laugh and a wave of her hand. It baffled Mark. To him, she was the most beautiful thing in existence. Her warmth, her kindness, her quick wit was everything he wanted.

Mark gave her a wet kiss on her cheek.

'Are you saying if it goes tits up, I need to fake my own death?' he asked.

'It's important to have a plan B. See, look.' She passed him the laptop.

The article explained that after an affair going sour and with mounting debt and a nasty drug addiction to boot, for John Stonehouse, the idea of jumping into the sea looked appealing.

'The slippery sod didn't even die. He sloped off to Australia and everything. They thought he was Lord Lucan when they found him,' Lucy added.

'They all do that now. I wonder if Carmichael will end up in the jungle. Similar in a way.'

The pair's laughter was interrupted by their plump ginger cat, Chunk, demanding attention and breakfast.

As Mark spooned out the congealed contents of the sachet a few minutes later, a thought popped into his head.

Meat for the grinder.

A couple of days later the thought was given substance. In a dour little room at the top of some stairs, in a back alley of Briarwood Town High Street, was the local Labour office. The light blinked as Mark sipped the fag ash masquerading as coffee. A man burst into the room and wasted no time barraging the would-be candidate.

'Mr Fallow, we like you. But I need to know now. Any skeletons? Closeted or not.'

This was Ren. The force of nature that had told Mark to meet here at 3 p.m. on Friday or the whole thing was off. Mark arrived promptly and the meeting commenced at 4:30 p.m.

'Nope. I've never murdered anyone!' Mark offered a joke.

Ren took off his spectacles and rubbed his face. 'Mr Fallow, I have over five hundred candidates to vet across the country. You want to become an MP, great. I'll give you a bit of advice, how about that? Jokes are no longer your friend. They are your worst fucking nightmare. Leave them to the speech writers. Humour is for humans, not politicians.'

The meeting lasted thirty minutes. It felt like three hundred. A rapid-fire grilling of epic proportions. Mark having to hold his hand up like scout's honour to affirm he wasn't into anything 'kinky'. Nor that any of his social media posts could come back to haunt him. This whole scenario was pitched as a consultation, a chance for the party brass to get to know their potential candidate better. It felt instead like an interrogation by an irritated bumblebee. Ren would slap his forehead and sigh at nearly every other word Mark offered. He felt terrible, sure that a rejection, an acme-style stamp would crash down onto his application with *DENIAL; FUCK OFF, MATE* stamped on it.

'So why do you want to do this, Mr Fallow? What are you all about?' Ren asked him after a question about if he'd ever defaced a mosque. (No, was the answer.)

What was Mark all about? That was the question. Every potential answer led back to Jackson Pierce.

Mark cocked his head, reaching deep for his *why*. 'Erm, mental health reform. More people to have more access more of the time?'

'Say *more* one *more* time, please.' Ren rolled his eyes.

'No, wait.' Mark stood up and paced in the little room. 'I just think it was such a struggle when I needed it. There were days, weeks where I wasn't sure what to do. And I had my wife, Lucy. What if you're alone? Who helps then?' Mark tapped the table to steady himself.

Ren didn't respond immediately. His glasses came off again, but this time he was slower, cleaning each lens with a cloth. 'It's a nice message, Mark, it really is.' Mark swelled a little inside. 'It's good as well because it's so wet, it won't overshadow Jackson. A damp jab rather than a knock-out punch.'

Jackson Pierce spoke about shattering tradition. His campaign didn't get bogged down in the details. As easy as breathing, he had melded the furore over Esther Murphy with the nation's distrust of the limping government.

'We need candidates like you. Jackson needs a foil. Congratulations—if your background checks come back, I think you're our guy for Briarwood. And a little birdie tells me the incumbent, that Lypton fella, he's truly snookered himself. Keep an eye on the news.'

'Thanks, Ren.'

'It's Renault to you.'

Mark sat back down, shellshocked. The reality was sinking in: he might win. An idea that was a mere pipedream a few days ago was now a seat within reach.

Mark Fallow was terrified, and still an overriding thought screamed at him.

Renault? What, like the fucking car?

3

As Mark scrambled to keep up, Jackson was ahead of the curve. With Renault working behind the scenes, Jackson could be the main event. The face of a new movement sweeping the country. He sat and surveyed the studio as people ferreted around.

Intimate, no desk, the chairs pulled closer.

Politicians always stood off, frequently hid.

No, they cowered behind rhetoric, even the past.

Not Jackson—he was here, on display for all to see.

'*And 3, 2, 1, live . . .* ' the director mouthed from just off camera.

Katie Turner was back in her usual habitat as the host of *Politics Live*. She sat across from him, ready to kick off as the show's credits finished rolling. Jackson found her attractive. Her short blonde bob framed her face better than any camera shot.

'Jackson Pierce, at the age of forty-four, in your first year of front-line politics, you are on the cusp of an unprecedented landslide election victory. All signs point to the fact you will be our next Prime Minister—'

'—We're changing that title.' Jackson nodded for her to continue.

'Okay, your withering assessment that the establishment is antiquated clearly resonates with voters.'

'Agreed.' He wafted a hand.

'Your policies are wildly popular, but some would argue there is a huge danger in changing so much in such a short time period. What do you say to those people?'

'That they're boring.'

'Sorry, that they're boring?'

'Yes. The usual answer would be people want change. But I think they want more than that. People want blood. Esther Murphy was a wake-up call. Carmichael, a bullet dodged. The electorate are sick of hearing that just because things have always been done like this, they must always be done like this. Well, I say no more.' Jackson held Katie's stare, letting his eyes bore into hers as a smile formed on his lips.

'And cut here. We'll pick it back up in a few minutes,' said the director.

Jackson straightened and glanced around at the various crew and onlookers in the buzzing studio. He brought his gaze back to Katie with a smirk. That had been a resounding success.

She was caught between a grimace and a frown. If Jackson had to guess, she was taken aback at his rhetoric. In time she would probably come to appreciate the boost in ratings.

Everyone was after some sort of gratification. Jackson had learnt many years ago as an orphan fending for himself that if you could home in on what that something was, you could win. Compromise was the language of a loser, and Jackson was no loser.

'You look a bit shocked, Katie.'

She fidgeted, leaning forward before she spoke.

'It's a bit dangerous, isn't it? *People want blood*. You're in a very influential position. Politicians don't talk like that.'

'Exactly. I'm not a politician, I'm a leader. I'm not lying to them, I'm not negotiating with them. I know what they want and I'll give it to them. That's why I'm going to win.'

'But at what cost?' Katie asked, distrust etched on her face.

'Sure, a marvellous question, if you choose to see the world that way'—Jackson swirled a finger before pointing it squarely at her—'but you've been close to the establishment for too long, Katie. You have to adapt or you're swept away. A lesson poor Belinda didn't learn.'

Unperturbed, Katie responded, 'In another time, the messages you're running on would be labelled as treasonous, Mr Pierce.'

She was biting; pity it was off camera. Smiling, he replied, 'Please call me Jackson.'

'No, thank you.'

'Oh, you're no fun. Look, not too long ago it was illegal to be gay, legal to smoke indoors and, even further back, you had to shit outside. The past is savagery, the present moderate.' Jackson leaned forward now to match her pose.

He continued, 'Change is scary when you're living through it. But after, when you look back, downright funny. I'm trying to expedite the process.'

'So what are you going to be called, then? The *Prime Minister* seems to have worked for everyone before you.'

'I think simply Leader.'

She paused, taking in what he had just said. She pressed her finger into her earpiece before speaking again.

'Right.' She grabbed a handful of her notes and broke Jackson's gaze. 'When we restart, I'll ask about some of these policy ideas. Perhaps *Workforce Growth*—is that okay? Or maybe *Fast-Track Food*? I would've run it by your Chief of Communications, but you don't have one.'

Jackson waved a hand as if unveiling himself. 'What you see is what you get. My message is simple. Everything is bogged down committees, helpers, hangers on. Politics has become slow, ponderous and broken. I'm here to blow it all away. Ask me whatever tickles your fancy, Katie; the people have made up their minds already.'

Katie went to speak again, but Jackson held up a solitary finger to quieten her. His phone buzzed in his pocket; Jackson got up and walked away. The director flapped his clipboard around as if he was having a stroke.

Jackson pulled out his phone and frowned at what he read. His mind raced to catch up, piecing together the implications as his thoughts scrambled. He gave a subtle nod, almost against his better judgement, then turned sharply and headed toward a big shiny door of the production room. The crew startled, but most froze, as if caught in the gravity of his presence.

He addressed them as friends, softening his stance, one hand slipping into his pocket. 'Guys, listen, this is going well—great, in fact!' He laughed, wandering over to the main desk.

He whipped around on his heels. 'But it could go better. I want everyone to see this. We need to capture their attention. People will watch the first few minutes of a political interview before drifting back to *EastEnders*. So when we restart, I'm giving Katie an exclusive.'

Before anyone could respond, Jackson turned and headed back to the studio. His smile disappeared the second he was through the door.

He slid his jacket off and ran his hands through his hair. Most women thought he had something of young Hugh Grant about him; he hated that idea, the glib buffoon.

He found himself staring at the striking birthmark on his left hand—the middle finger, to be exact. If he squinted, it looked almost like a star. The newspapers had picked up on it, saying he had a starry touch.

'We'll start up in thirty seconds,' the director shouted.

He found Katie where he had left her, preparing for round

two. She shot him a smile, insincere no doubt. 'A little birdie tells me you've got something special for us now, Mr Leader, sir.'

'You do have a sense of humour. I was beginning to worry,' Jackson said as he sat down, thinking back to the text on the phone.

'*And 3, 2, 1, live,*' mouthed the director.

Jackson was ready to change the game.

London hummed that evening. Incandescent light poured from streetlights and car headlamps, giving vivid brightness to the noise of the city. The backlit Houses of Parliament stood solemn, Big Ben ever watchful overhead. Jackson's forehead pressed harder against the window of his chauffeur-driven car; he didn't want the Houses to slip out of view as the car lurched around the bend.

The news bulletin on the radio babbled about his showing on *Politics Live*. Jackson's political opponents probably couldn't fathom why he had done it. There was a book on how to run a general election campaign, but Jackson Pierce was watching a film instead.

He was miles ahead in the polls; the election was next week. It was a done deal, yet he felt the need to open himself up to more comment, more column inches, and to Katie Turner no less, hardly a shrinking violet.

He had to admit that on first reading of the text message, he was sceptical. Too much risk; too much, too soon. As he processed the words, however, he decided the instruction to announce his intention to dissolve the House of Lords was genius.

The Commons and the Lords went together like chalk and cheese in Jackson's eyes. Britain didn't need a two-House system anymore. If the Crown accepted its ceremonial position, then the Lords was on borrowed time.

Funny to think that the Upper Chamber had been the preeminent power centre in British politics for centuries, the Commons little more than a junior partner. A call back to an era when status was determined by the amount of land held or who your father was. The fact it could still play a pivotal role in legislative matters was a farce.

Of course it had immediately created an uproar. But dinosaurs probably cried out too, screamed in panic as the meteor crashed down, as ash swallowed them up.

As Jackson saw it, this was the weakness of the establishment, with all of their rules and traditions. They were so comfortable with centuries of inertia that when hit squarely on the nose, there was no instinct to fight back, only scream.

He glanced at the speech again, the words that had flowed on television.

'As Leader, I will dissolve the House of Lords. A symbol for the stagnation of our country. I am an orphan, a child made possible by the power of the state. There is no place in my society for nepotism, for hereditary gifts.

For too long have people's futures been dictated by this country's past. Believe me, this is not the end but just the start of what we will do. Democracy has lost its meaning. I intend to deliver it back to the people.

If you've already decided to vote for me, then thank you. If you haven't, then we don't need you. Stay in the past. Stay in the dark. The future begins now.'

Katie Turner had sat mouth agape at this pronouncement. Jackson thought he could hear the bleating of the producers buzzing out of her earpiece to say something, anything. He didn't care; he had simply walked away and into the waiting car.

There had been some insinuation, some hints that Jackson had radical policy ideas, but they hadn't been set in stone until tonight. Well, now they knew—now they all knew.

Election night was less than a week away, and their plan was right on track.

THE ELECTION

Breaking News: Prime Minister's Questions? What does the first week of a Pierce Premiership look like? As latest poll shows, dissolution of House of Lords has overwhelming public support

4

The razor-thin line between collaboration and exploitation is ignorance. Mark walked it as well as he could, but even the most adept trapeze artist could fall. As he and Lucy got out of the car at a little after nine in the evening, he couldn't afford to look down.

Polls closed in an hour, and a nervous energy had swept the country as it woke up that Thursday. It was election day.

Mark's life had been a whirlwind since securing the candidacy. Renault made sure the rookie attended all sorts of civic engagements; Mark was never more than a couple of inches from a microphone's muff. It was a chance to patent his patter: mental health reform, working hard for the sleepy Hertfordshire seat of Briarwood and perhaps even the bin days. Instead, it became an exercise in avoidance. The news cycle focused on questions of dog's paws and how handsome Jackson really was.

It was the first of these topics that Mark hoped to avoid as they approached the two men perched on the walls on either side of the entrance to Briarwood Community Centre. Every so often, they would quieten down to check someone's ID. Mark gripped Lucy's hand tighter the closer they got.

'But if there was a gun to your head, Mike,' the man on the left said before taking a big hit of his vape. A smell of damp peaches drifted over.

Mike let out a big sigh. 'This is stupid. You're asking me to choose between *Gavin and Stacey* or people's health.'

'Yeah, but I read somewhere that we'd be much better off without the NHS—waiting times, you know. The middle managers suck all the money up. I'll send you the link.'

'It's not like there's a slider in Downing Street that says *"fund the World Service"* on one end and *"fix people for free"* on the other.'

'What's the *World Service*? Anyway, it's the sort of thing Jackson will fix. He'll make the right call.'

'Which is?' Mike asked in a deeply disinterested monotone.

Chris didn't have an answer at first. 'Hmm, maybe bin both of them. I got TV on my phone, haven't I? And I'll just get private medical insurance.'

'And you can afford that, can you?'

'If they stop taxing me to pay for the NHS, and with no licence fee, then sure, probably, definitely. Yeah.'

Mike was still scrunching his face as Mark fumbled for his passport at the front of the queue.

'I'm standing. My name is Mark Fallow. This is my wife, Lucy.'

Chris piped up at the sound of Mark's name.

'Mike, ask him. What would he do? What would you do, Mr Fallow?'

It was the man behind that saved Mark from answering. In retrospect more flung him from the frying pan into the fire.

'A comment on the record for your opponent's poor foot-work, Mr Fallow?' The man's journalist credentials swung loosely from his jacket as his phone made clear it was listening.

Mark didn't respond. Renault had told him under no circumstances to engage or, even worse, try to make light of his opponent's situation.

Chester Lypton's misstep was his and his alone. He was the long-serving incumbent for Briarwood. Ripe to be put to pasture, a stoic, dependable Middle-England career politician. Cut him and he'd bleed blue Conservative. And in the wake of

Carmichael's political kamikaze, cut him they did; people were hungry for another witch hunt.

Rabid little shit, his paw, his paw-paw . . . blared the viral remix. Renault had even cracked a smile when showing Mark. The looping footage of this most boring man fiddling with his glasses, his cheeks reddening to a heady crimson. An accidental step on a guide dog's paw while rushing past constituents after a heated surgery.

It might have blown over, but Lypton's tone-deaf apology reignited the blaze. Before he could say *unreservedly*, the internet had crowned him the Tory that hurts dogs.

The question was repeated. The men vetting the IDs stopped. Mark was stuck in the queue to his future with a live hand grenade in his lap. Lucy tugged gently, urging him to move. But Mark was steadfast, and in hindsight, stupid.

'Yes, of course.' He opened his arms like he thought politicians should. 'It's unfortunate. But in the grand scheme of things, it's not as if he stepped on a voter—or an immigrant.'

The journalist's eyes narrowed. He shifted his weight in excitement.

'Mr Fallow, did you just compare immigrants to dogs?'

'No! Wait. Is this on the record? Can we go off? How does it work?'

Mark stepped towards him in a panic. He came down hard on the journalist's foot.

'Ow, Christ!' The journalist lurched as he went backwards and knocked into Chris on the wall, who was mid-pull on his peachy vape. Arms went up as the plastic stick seemed to float in the air amidst its own haze.

Mark reacted, trying to catch Chris. All he got for his trouble was a kick in the face as Chris windmilled his way over the wall.

Mark reeled as Lucy came to him. He was fine; it smarted but nothing more than a scrape.

'Oh, it's going to be a black eye, alright,' Lucy said quietly.

'A black eye!' Mark shouted in distress.

Chris was up, dusting himself down. The journalist was laughing, and a little crowd had gathered to see the commotion.

'That'll make a lovely photo.' The journalist raised his phone and snapped.

Mike was laughing his head off, watching Chris look for his vape somewhere in the dark. 'Cor, you need some media training, Mr Fallow.'

'Or bloody ballet lessons,' Chris muttered.

The journalist was tapping at his phone as he wandered away. Mark was frozen to the spot. It was Lucy who got him moving again, whispering, 'Come, let's go inside. We'll deal with whatever that was later.'

Mark felt figuratively and physically beaten already and he hadn't even stepped inside the main hall yet.

'Fuck sake. All that because I'm terrified to answer.'

'It's a learning curve. It will come. It all depends on what type of politician you want to be.'

'Universally loved and respected?'

Lucy raised a hand in a calming gesture. 'Let's start with just not a clumsy cockwomble, yeah?'

Mark nodded. 'Deal. Why'd I have to say immigrants anyway?'

The hall was awash with motion. Busy people rushed around, the majority wearing trainers, as if doing a fitness test. In comparison, the candidates stood out by their polished shoes. Like bird watching, Mark saw a lesser spotted Chester Lypton in the corner, chatting easily with a group of people.

Glenda Trywhitt, the sole surviving Liberal Democrat candidate in Hertfordshire, was moving around the room, shaking as many hands as she could. Perhaps a five-pound note in each clasp. No sign of the Loony Party candidate, but you never knew if Viscount Soup would turn up at these things anymore. He was getting on a bit.

Lucy nodded towards the back of the hall. The stage with two massive flat-screen televisions hanging above it. They flared into life as Jackson's face beamed down in stereo. It was the news, the two indistinguishable nowadays. He appeared outside his own counting hall in Lambeth. The volume was pumped up and the community centre fell silent as everyone flocked to watch.

'Mr Pierce—'

'Call me Jackson.'

'Jackson, we are a few minutes away from the all-important exit poll. Is it fair to say you're another step closer to visiting the King?'

'I could just send the King a text, couldn't I?' Jackson laughed, probably not joking. 'I have my agenda ready to go, the first bills ready to push forward. But we must wait.'

'It's tradition, asking the King to form a government.'

Jackson pursed his lips. The reporter had said the trigger word.

'Tradition, yes. We used to fox hunt, didn't we? That was tradition. Or "penny for the guy". Remember that? Maybe we can take the vote back off women. Tradition for tradition's sake. Slippery slope, no?'

The poor reporter was clearly stunned.

There was a tap on Mark's shoulder. 'I tell you what, I thought stepping on that damn dog's paw was the worst thing that could have happened to me. Now I'm not so sure.'

It was Chester Lypton, the incumbent. He gestured to the screen. The balding bespectacled man stood a similar height to Mark and was extending his hand.

'Mr Lypton, hello. Pleasure to meet you.'

'Pleasure's all mine, Mr Fallow, really it is.' He pointed to Mark's eye. 'Been busy, I see.'

'Bruising, this job, right?'

Lypton laughed. 'Twenty years I've been an MP. I don't think I'd last twenty minutes under Pierce. Congratulations.'

Mark was unsure how to respond.

Chester leaned in, his voice dropping. 'Allow me the indulgence of imparting some wisdom. You'll need something to set you apart. A platform. You don't want to just be part of the crowd. Jackson's got his plans, but at the start he'll need his MPs; he'll need allies. You need to find your own way in.'

He smiled with consummate ease before stepping back with a quick glance at the busy room. 'You'll figure it out, I'm sure.'

'How do you mean?'

'Let's just say . . . you want to be in the tent pissing out . . . pardon my French. Good luck with your speech.'

Ever the veteran politician, he drifted back into the maelstrom of people, leaving Mark and Lucy silent.

'What a strange man. About to lose his job and he was happy,' Lucy said.

Just after ten o'clock the exit poll was expected, usually the first clear sign of which way the country was heading. This time to clarify how large the margin would be.

Mark sat there fidgeting, rolling his pen back and forth along his thigh. The volume rose on the TVs again; the exit polls were in.

'We are projecting over five hundred . . .'

Mark didn't hear the rest of the sentence, for the roar that followed Katie Turner announcing that Pierce was on course for over five hundred MPs was deafening. Mark looked up to the roof, as if it were about to fly off any second.

Jackson was always going to win, that was accepted. But this was the obliteration of the Conservative Party. Less than fifty MPs returned when all was said and done.

'Wow. Nowhere to hide now, is there?' Lucy said.

Mark stared at his boss on the TV. They were showing images live from Lambeth as Jackson paced like a tiger in a zoo. 'It's his way or the highway. He can do anything he wants with that sort of majority.'

Lucy grabbed his hand. 'For sure, but let's start smaller, at home. What do *you* want?'

'Do I have a choice?'

'Everyone has a choice. My advice would be to look at everything on its merits before you vote.'

'A lovely idea, but I can't. I have to vote with whatever Jackson wants me to. Actually, maybe that's my niche—the first bastard to dissent. Revolution on revolution.'

'I'd vote for you.' She winked at him. 'Look, it feels big, but don't forget, it's been a success tonight. You're going to be an MP. Congratulations.'

It was a formality in the end. An hour later, Mark found himself on stage, flanked by Lypton and Glenda of the Lib Dems. An excellent name for a band, Mark thought.

Mark Fallow was returned as the Member for Briarwood for the Labour Party, with 22,673 votes, a 62% share.

As the returning officer stepped away from the microphone and the applause died down, it was Mark's moment to announce himself to his new constituents. His chest tightened as he repeated the opening line in his head.

Good evening, Briarwood. Sorry Jackson couldn't be here tonight, but he sent me instead. I am Mark Fallow and I am proud to be your Member of Parliament.

Mark approached the microphone. He raised it, because he was a foot taller than the returning officer. Pausing for a moment, he looked back at Lucy, who was standing off to his right, beaming at him.

'Good evening, Briarwood.'

He was interrupted by a shout from the crowd. 'Pierce is making a big announcement!'

Before Mark could do anything, the TVs were back on and the volume blasted up. Jackson's dulcet tones flooded the hall.

' . . . yes, well, as I said, we've wasted time confirming the result. I want to get to work, oh, and I have some updates on what we'll be starting with.'

'An exclusive?' The reporter was hopeful.

'If you like. The Labour Party doesn't work for us. Not for this new movement. This is a promise. A promise that I've made to the people of Britain. I've thought about it and I want the history books to show a new era. So when we look at the Workforce Growth and the Lords Dissolution bills tomorrow, we will do so as a new party. The Pierce Promise.'

'Can you just do that?'

'I just did.'

And with that, no one cared Mark was on stage or what he had to say. That wasn't strictly true. Mark felt a ping in his pocket. He saw Lucy look at her own phone too. A notification from X.

'Briarwood MP Fallow compares immigrants to dogs.' Accompanied by a photo of a red and swollen-eyed Mark.

As he stood there, face swelling further, Mark realised he was just a cog in the machine of over five hundred MPs for Jackson Pierce.

He drifted away, off stage and back to Lucy.

'There's always your maiden speech in the Commons. Can you repurpose some of it?' Lucy said.

Mark felt his phone buzz again, no doubt Renault with some choice words.

'Oh yeah, Parliament—the tent Lypton was talking about.'

Mark sighed and gently probed his sore face.

Now, like many men his age, he had to figure out how to piss in the right direction.

5

ark's eye may have been shining brightly, but Jackson had the spotlight firmly on him. The two men shared a room for the first time. The House was full, the green benches of the Commons lost under a sea of drab suits.

Every single MP Jackson commanded, and even the scant few he didn't, were here. The tension and anticipation for his first *Prime Minister's Questions* had built by that Wednesday, a mere six days after the election.

Jackson approached the raggedy old despatch box, placing his phone on it so it was in view. The hanging microphones swayed from the sheer volume of MPs packed inside the Commons like sardines, shuffling and wheezing, coughing and turning. Ahead of him to his right, a man stood, after the raffling of papers had died down. He asked a question, directing it at Jackson.

'Does the Prime Minister actually have a belief system or is he just sounding off platitudes and governing on the basis of whatever will make him most popular?'

He looked the man up and down; his name was Stuart Gallows, one of the few Conservatives left, a real vocal piece of work. The sort that pretended to know the price of a pint of milk.

Sarcasm flecked Jackson's voice. 'I thank the Honourable Gentleman, from one of the constituencies that really should have known better than to elect him, for his question. And I simply ask, what does it matter?'

A roar erupted from both sides of the House. The Speaker, Rachel Jenkins, shuffled in her chair and was about to stand to bring order. Rules were rules, and Jackson must play by them, that would be her line. Except Jackson didn't want to. He shouldn't have to.

He glared at the Speaker and continued.

'No. In fact, I think the Honourable Gentleman – No, do you know what, let's just use names. Stuart.'

A silence where Jackson expected further thunder. He was betraying centuries worth of rules and traditions. You didn't name a member of the House. Only the Speaker could do that, and only when rebuking them under punishment of sanction or even suspension.

Jackson's phone buzzed. He glanced down at the screen. Six words.

Stay calm. Jenkins wavers. Push back.

Sure enough, the silence was punctured by the booming voice of Madam Speaker. She shouted, 'Order! The Prime Minister will respect the rules and traditions of this chamber.'

'Or what, Rachel?'

'You will be ejected and this session will be adjourned.'

'You would deny the country a chance to have their Leader speak? An opportunity to hear him explain how he wants to help them?'

She was caught off guard by this retort, stuttering, 'Well, no, but . . .'

Jackson smiled. 'I will carry on. After all, I have the largest mandate ever given to a winner of a general election. Times are changing, and I am here now. Hush.'

Another message. Jackson again glanced down at his phone.

> Challenge them. Remind them what you're here to do.

Turning his attention again to the windbag Stuart, Jackson's confidence built.

'My belief system is that I do not want to see another Esther Murphy die. I don't want regular British people to feel the pinch when they go to the shops. Entrepreneurs and business owners should be able to follow their dreams without hindrance. I want common sense and modernity to take precedence.'

A loud roar from his supporting MPs. He glanced at what was left of the Opposition. Hanging on like cockroaches, he thought.

'This is the end of traditions for tradition's sake. This Chamber, a sorry old dusty relic, is a prime example of why I stand here today charged with blowing the cobwebs away.'

The Speaker was forlorn, the reality of her true position and power sinking in.

'Whether you believe in me as a man of my convictions or not, frankly it's rain in the wind. The House of Lords is going; the House of Commons is changing. Britain does not want to waste time on the politics of old. One party rules, another throws barbs. They swap. Rinse and repeat. It's a played-out dance for a played-out era. Red blames blue, the incumbent points at the predecessor, until the cycle comes round to their exit, and it all starts all over again. All the while, nothing gets done. We go left, we go right, and we end up back at square one.'

A notification on his phone flashed up.

Announce t now.

'Starting next week, we will begin fast tracking our bills through. To mark the start of our plans, I am announcing a new cryptocurrency, the *Pierce£*. Each member of the public that committed to the Pierce Promise at the election will receive a starting value of coins worth £5,000. If you didn't vote for me, then better luck next time.'

Jackson let that land. Shock and calculation on people's faces and in their heads. He'd been assured it was financially feasible, technically viable, and he would worry about the implications of it later.

Cries from the decimated opposition, maybe even a few of his own MPs, he didn't know or care.

'That's unconstitutional!'

'It's illegal, isn't it?'

'What, like Bitcoin?'

'We didn't sign up for this.'

Jackson paused. Sure enough, the phone received another message. He smirked as he read it.

Show me where.

'Unconstitutional? Illegal? Show me on the constitution where that can't be done. Oh right, that's it, there isn't one. It's not written down anywhere. Another of our wonderful dichotomies, a place of consistency and tradition based on nothing but the word of honourable gentlemen. Nonsense.'

Rachel Jenkins screamed for order. 'The Prime Minister will cease this line of argument. The constitution may be unwritten, but it is enforced by precedent and law. You are bound by—'

'Law? Precedent?' Jackson interjected. 'Take it to court, see how long it takes to get moving. Your world view is built on the idea that we all play fair—which is just a lie. Tell me,

Rachel, what happens when the game you are playing is over? From now your authority reaches as far as I say it does.'

This had gone about as well as he could have hoped. Now for the finale.

'My advice to you all is that you need to adapt—or you will cease. This is my first and last PMQs. I communicate with the people, not play politics in this dilapidated temple of antiquity that accepts lies as currency. I offer new currency now—the Pierce Promise.'

Jackson walked away, a furious murmur carrying through the Commons. The House was divided; there was uproar everywhere. Passing the Speaker's chair, he winked at Rachel. She stared back in shock.

She looked like her world had just ended. Jackson supposed it had.

6

The benefit of having a rockstar with a messiah complex for a boss was that the fallout from Mark's gaffe on election night could have been worse. It wasn't great still—people thought he was a wanker mere minutes into the job—but hey, that was politics.

Still, Mark had some mending to do and, courtesy of the rollicking afforded by Renault, today was a very good time to start. Mark was working from home. Not quite an office, it was the spare bedroom. Complete with its peeling wallpaper and cracked skirting board.

Jackson's first (and last) PMQs had diverted attention. Mark had been there, stuffed onto the backbenches, claustrophobia pairing well with Jackson's fledgling constitutional crisis. It put paid to any notion that Mark's maiden speech would be any time soon. The Commons retreated and licked its wounds; there were challenges, appeals, even talk of court action against Pierce. He had just laughed and carried on anyway.

The door creaked open and Lucy entered with some toast and a huge coffee. 'Here,' she said, placing it on his uneven desk. 'You might need to inject it today.'

He sighed, rubbing a hand over his face. Today was all about showing how he could 'bounce back' and that he had some 'gumption'. The words from Lypton had also sunk in. Mark needed a platform. Ideally one that would allow him to, on Renault's insistence, 'clean his own fucking mess up'.

His phone buzzed on the desk. Renault had obliged with multiple media opportunities. A reminder flashed about his slot on Emma Trent's Breakfast Show in thirty minutes, followed by an interview with a local paper. He couldn't shake the feeling that he'd been dropped into the deep end. At least the black eye had faded.

'You know, I reckon a coffee machine that poured it straight into your eyeballs would go down a storm on *Dragons' Den*,' Lucy said from her seat on the edge of the tiny bed as she gulped from her own cup.

Mark laughed. 'Peter Jones would go for it, but I imagine Bartlett would want to know about your social media exposure.'

'Compostable coffee pods to go with it—that will hook Deborah in. One Dragon is all I need.' She shimmied round the crap on the floor and placed a hand on Mark's shoulder. 'You'll get a chance for your maiden speech, I promise. Jackson just needs to throw his toys around a bit before anyone else can play with them.'

'It wasn't a complete washout. I managed to see the little post office they have in Parliament—oh, and someone told me about some hidden passageway they found a few years ago. I'm basically an expert now.'

Lucy changed the subject with a squeeze of his shoulder.

'What's the plan with Emma Trent? Music that Moves You!'

Lucy mimed a little dance; the jingle for the Breakfast Show was a high-pitched monstrosity and played every twenty seconds.

'Fuck sake, what if she asks what *moves me*?'

'Erm, you can tell her, erm . . . that you want to get the buses moving on time?'

'Okay, we're done here.' Mark pointed to the door.

'I kid, I kid. You'll be fine. You know what a Swiftie is, right?'

Mark gulped hard.

'I'm to expect blowback on the immigrant comment. Renault says to go straight. Route one. I misspoke, it was an intense day, and it shouldn't distract from the job at hand. Delivering on the Pierce Promise. Beyond that, he said to absolutely have fun with it.'

'Did he?' Lucy raised an eyebrow.

'Nope. Of course not. I'm to suffocate it and not shit the bed any further. His exact words.' Mark let out a sigh as he swivelled in the rickety desk chair, his knees bobbing under the desk. 'It's pointless anyway. She's just going to want to talk about Jackson. He's overshadowing every other topic. The media is obsessed with his antics. I can't remember the last time we spoke about anything other than the House of Lords or what he was going to do next.'

'You just need to forget him today. In this room Jackson Pierce does not exist. If they ask about him, steer it back to what you want to say.'

Mark wanted to talk about mental health, about his plans for a new drop-in clinic and a new twenty-four-hour helpline staffed by real people who understood OCD.

'You're right.'

'I know I'm right. You've got a story to tell; you've been on a *"journey"*, as the kids say nowadays. Tell it.'

He closed his eyes and found himself back on that plane. Mark was there, sitting on the emergency exit row; he was over six feet tall and valued the extra leg space.

An unmistakable belief had consumed him. He was about to stand up and rip open the door. Thirty-five thousand feet in the air, an uneventful commuter flight from Belfast back to Luton. A mundane sales trip for his job at a software company. And Mark Fallow was about to end it all. For himself and for everyone else onboard.

He spent the rest of the flight sweating, willing himself to look away from the door. His knuckles whitened as he gripped his seat as hard as he could, as if about to be ripped away by someone, when it was himself he was frightened of.

'Remember that's why you're doing it.' Lucy placed a hand on his back. Mark opened his eyes.

She was right; that was where this had all started. Everyone struggles with unwanted thoughts or ideas and images that are uncomfortable. But for most, they flicker just for a moment before fading. Mark's thoughts dance cruelly, painting the walls of his mind, replaying again and again. Lurid, disgusting scenarios that play on fear, attacking the things a person loves the most in this world.

The diagnosis came swiftly after that flight. His anxiety was rooted in OCD, a particular form that manifested in the main via intrusive thoughts. He would never have opened that door, acted on any of his dark compulsions, in fact, and he had spent every day since then trying to cling to that truth.

Lucy disappeared for a second and returned with a folder. She handed it to Mark with two hands. 'And if you need some inspiration, I knocked this up for you last night.'

Surprised, Mark took the folder and opened it. Notes, newspaper cuttings, highlighted anecdotes and ideas for his media day. Even a page of 'acceptable Dad jokes'. He was in awe of her.

He felt emotion rise in his chest. He stood to embrace his wife, hitting his knees on the way up. The desk bucked like a horse.

'Okay, but what is a Swiftie? Thanks, I love you,' he whispered as he hugged her.

'You're welcome.' She laughed, leaning in to kiss his cheek. 'Now go and show them who you are.'

~

The first interview wasn't complete hell. Emma Trent was a bundle of energy but Mark managed to keep pace, a slightly duller foil for her slick, carefree persona. The chat lurched uncomfortably to election night. Mark handled it well. Emma accepted that people could misspeak. Inevitably it then took a turn towards Jackson, but Mark managed to rescue it and steer the conversation towards mental health and the people of Briarwood.

He had a small gap now before his interview with the local paper, and he allowed himself a chocolate digestive and another cup of coffee. He balled his feet up on the carpet like that scene in *Die Hard* and for a second he was John McClane in every discernible way.

Mark's phone started to flash, his do not disturb screening calls but allowing anything from Lucy . . . or Renault.

'Fallow. Clear your schedule. I have something special for you.' Renault's words had a physical quality to them, Mark thought.

'Sure. I'm free after the paper.'

'Splendid, and would sir like lunch on the veranda? No, you pillock, cancel the paper. You're free as of now. It's at quarter past.'

'Okay, sorry, sure. What's the plan?'

'To mop up the puddle of piss you left on your first day in big boy pants. The local stuff is too . . . local. *This Morning* will break you in. Sink or swim. I imagine you used armbands for a long time.'

Until thirteen—specialist armbands, Mark thought ashamedly.

'Thought you said quarter past twelve? Who's it with?'

'*This Morning*.'

'Fuck.'

'There we are. Less of the potty mouth. One of the producers is an old friend. Turns out they're interested in who

Pierce's new lot are. The idea is to showcase a *"lesser* known MP" and I couldn't think of anyone *lesser*. I've got to go, but I'll send you the details in a minute. And Fallow?'

'Yes, Renault.'

'Don't fuck it up.'

The biggest daytime television show in the country—a show that made people into household names.

Mark was stunned. He wanted a platform; here it was.

THE INCIDENT

Breaking News: Genius or Criminal? The realities behind the Pierce£ coins — is #CryptoVoting the future?

7

Mark would, much later, think it quite a novel experience to see himself masturbate on the internet. As he was about to rearrange himself, he had no idea that the next few minutes would shape everything that followed. Perfect ignorance was perfect bliss, at the time.

When he watched it back, he would notice the disturbing angles first. A director's cut of his own private habits. His chin looked spotty, but his eyes—those were the worst. He would compare them to those of dogs when hunting foxes. Illegal, unethical looks. The stream was even kind enough to provide the context of his misdeeds.

He would later remember the sound of Lucy almost breaking down the door. The thud of her bag being flung onto the table, then her hurried steps on the stairs, quieter with distance.

By the time the door to the box room opened, he would be numb.

His worst nightmare made real.

But that was later.

Mark crushed it. He settled into a nice rhythm on *This Morning*. It was only a five-minute segment, but it felt like an eternity.

Renault sent him a short review.

Christ, you're dull.

Flipping over to socials, he saw #FallowMP trending at number 37. The pick of the comments read, 'He seems decent, for a politician.' *Small victories.*

Now alone in the house after Lucy went into work, the decision was made—he deserved a pizza for his lunch. Mark watched as the little AI bot whizzed around. It told him all the steps that went into his afternoon nap inducer. It dawned on him that it wasn't a bad idea for the government, to be honest; maybe Jackson should create something like this:

Step 1 Policy Drafted
Step 2 Baked Under Scrutiny in the Commons
Step 3 All Toppings Removed

Probably replacing them with vegan cheese or just sand. That represented the compromises that were needed to get it done. Step 4 and beyond was where the analogy really fell apart. A more complex description was needed for the utter ball-breaking boredom that came next for getting bills passed into law.

Wait, that's not right. Jackson's would be a lot cleaner:

Step 1 We're doing this
Step 2 It's done
Step 3 Fuck off

Mark's phone pinged. It was Renault again, this time with an instruction.

'Check out the Mail Online.'

Forcing himself to the website, sure enough, there it was. *'Fallow Fires on This Morning'*.

He scanned the recap of his performance. It focused quite a lot on what Alison, the presenter, was wearing, but the bits about Mark were . . . there, he supposed.

'A happily married man.'

'Someone with their head screwed on.'

These were just simple facts to Mark.

But maybe it was going well? Mark had worked hard on himself the past few years. He'd developed a bunch of mechanisms that helped him reset and purge his mind when the thoughts intruded. Planning his words and speeches was one. Escaping into a book or a movie another. Whilst the third was more raw.

Masturbation was natural.

It was something we all did, and if not, we should. Learning more about the scientific benefits of it, as part of his counselling, was eye-opening for Mark. If it were a Yakult it wouldn't even be a consideration. But it was still something of a taboo, certainly among British men, and more so among politicians. Still, here Mark was, looking to unwind after a successful yet stressful morning. According to the little pizza robot, his food was a while off, and with the house to himself an urge . . . emerged.

Oxytocin, serotonin and endocannabinoids were all words Mark would say if ever confronted over this particular coping mechanism. While the exact science slipped his mind, he hoped if he said the words loud enough and with enough authority, someone else would fill in the blanks.

His first mistake was clicking onto the picture. His eyes were drawn to the article above his on the right-hand side. Soapstar Jill Bradshaw on holiday in Tenerife. Jill was cavorting in a bikini, frolicking in the water. He should have clicked off, but a candle still burnt for Jill. Men of his vintage remembered her heyday in the early noughties.

Mark's second mistake was being happy. In that microcosm, he was relaxed and content. The hyper-worried, always-anxious Mark was replaced by this most normal of chirpy blokes. It was this second mistake that snowballed into the third and final.

Somewhere in the corner of his eye, Mark's subconscious probably noticed the red light. Perhaps his ears even caught the quiet notification sound that he'd connected back up to the live feed of ITV's main broadcast.

But as blood redistributed itself, Mark turned over his phone and was blissfully ignorant of the reality around him. There was only Jill. A private tender climax of an unrequited teenage crush.

As if rewarding his exertion, the doorbell went.

Mark pulled up his pants and went to answer the door.

'Sorry, sorry, I'm coming!'

The delivery guy—Scott from his name badge—had a huge grin on his face. His eyes flared as the door opened, and Mark was struck with the idea that this man well and truly adored his job. Good for him, he thought.

'You just have, haven't you?'

Mark scrunched his face in confusion.

Scott ripped open the foil bag, saying, 'Hope you've washed your hands, mate,' before handing him the sweaty boxes.

'You know, I voted for you, for Jackson really, but yeah, good to see you in action just now. Sticking it to . . . well, you know.'

'Thanks very much. It's been a lot this past week. Hungry for more, if you excuse the terrible pun. Do you have the extra garlic sauce I ordered?' Mark noticed the hole it usually filled was very much empty.

'Yeah, sorry, mate—never enough, is there?' He found it crushed at the bottom of the bag and passed it to Mark.

Pizza secured and Scott dispatched, Mark turned to the kitchen to plate up. In the privacy of his own home, Mark the MP would start as he meant to go on. Proper crockery.

He could hear the buzzing of his phone, left in a rush to answer the door, on his desk. That meant it had to be Lucy or Renault. Neither a good idea to ignore, but the grumble in his stomach made a good argument. Listen to all sides of the debate; consider all issues on merit.

It was on the third bite of the first slice sat at his desk that Mark decided to flip his phone over. A swipe of his greasy finger left a smear; the image on X left a wound that would last a lifetime. At first it was surreal. But the subconscious has a way of screaming. Mark felt his stomach lurch before his cognitive load had even processed what he was looking at.

Thirty-two notifications from Renault. Nineteen from Lucy. Countless never-ending pings on X and Facebook as his phone felt like it was experiencing its very own Chernobyl. A meltdown of Mark's life. Clipped, streamed, posted and aggregated before Mark could even consider the wedges that drooped with a sad sog on his plate.

The door downstairs was almost blown off its hinges. A scream in the distance came. 'Mark! The fucking webcam. Turn it off!'

She knew it was too late, and so did Mark. Everyone knew it now.

Mark sat defeated, distraught and doused in his own tears. It was Lucy, the ever-dependable love of his life, that had to swallow her own rage, her own embarrassment, and pick up the pieces.

#Wankgate, #OnlyFallow, and just plain simple #WankMP were trending in grim unison. Mark had excelled. From #37 to #1. Jackson—for once—wasn't the story. Every refresh brought new posts: screenshots, memes and commentary from people who were far too quick with Photoshop.

Scandal invited opinion, and it flowed freely from the usual suspects.

Mark finally spoke. 'Is it bad?'

Lucy took a deep breath. 'It's popular. Put it that way.'

'I've invented a whole new category of shame.' Mark rolled back into a ball.

Jill Bradshaw posted about it. Lorraine Kelly as well, so too Alison and Dermot from *This Morning*. Unilaterally denouncing the objectification of women but agreeing that Jill absolutely should be a guest soon.

Mark put his hands over his face. 'I was stressed. I did a good job. It's natural; it's not illegal. Has Jackson posted anything yet?'

'I don't think so. He's probably got bigger things to be getting on with. His bill for starters—the *Workforce Growth* thingy.'

Mark wasn't listening. 'Why didn't I notice the webcam?'

'Come on let me make you a cup of tea.'

Mark felt like babbling: the images, Renault, Jackson. Instead he unfurled slowly and took her hand. 'I'm sorry, Lucy. I've ruined it, everything we worked so hard on the past year. How on earth can I go into Parliament and look anyone straight in the eye? I will forever be *that* guy who did *that* thing.'

'One day at a time. We can get through this.' A buzzing cut through Lucy's words.

And here he was: Ren.

Mark debated peeking at the message. In the end he had to rip the Band-Aid off. There were many, each insult, each tirade more colourful than the last. It was the most recent, the end of the communications, that Mark felt most keenly in his gut.

You're a fucking wanker, Fallow.

Yep. Well done, Mark.

8

The Right Members Club watched on, curious. Mark Fallow presented something of an opportunity. But their due diligence had to be spotless. See, even for a secret society that recruited disgraced MPs, they had standards.

'Well—' Zachary stroked his chin, hamming it up '—there was the junior Minister that was caught watching porn in the Commons, not once, mind, but twice!'

'He wasn't engaging, as it were, if I remember correctly,' Susie said.

'You're right. His todger was firmly on the backbenches.'

William overheard the debate. He had asked his Members to dig. The Club was meant to have a full complement of seven, though it was hardly a first-come-first-serve arrangement. He resisted making that particular pun. Each Member was chosen according to their sin, and it had to be a truly singular one that had brought about their fall from grace.

Take Zachary—Member for Gluttony. Cocaine in the toilets of Parliament. Pissed-up most sessions, and a liability for the party whip. William wasted no time in inducting him after Zachary missed a crucial vote on the war in Iraq. His ability to mingle and befriend, a drink in each hand, meant he was a crucial weapon in William's arsenal.

Now, as William poured himself a pint and surveyed the room, he felt quietly satisfied with his charges: Gluttony, Pride,

Greed, Sloth and Envy—each a disaster in their own right, yet together the perfect complement to his own sin: Wrath.

'Lust is a tricky one. The further you go back, it's all just affairs and lurid trysts. It's too espionage. Too *From Russia with Love*.' Jessica pushed her book away from her with a sigh.

'Fawkes didn't have this problem. Precedence,' Derek mumbled, his Geordie accent making the syllables of the last word sing.

'I can tell you now, without getting papercuts from those relics, no one in the long and *un*storied history of this Club has been inducted on account of pleasuring themselves in front of the whole nation—hell, the entire world!' Susie said.

'Pierce is unchecked. We haven't been able to make a dent. Are you sure this kinky Fallow bastard is the answer?' Jessica asked.

'He's the key,' William said, certainty in his voice.

Everyone nodded. The boss had spoken. Horace grabbed an armful of dusty books. 'This is the last of it. I've searched every shelf in the archive. Every Member, going back to 1605 and the plot.'

'Is this really necessary, William?' Zachary asked, his head dropping at the sight of Horace's bundle. 'If he's our guy, our seventh Member, can't we just get on with it?'

William held a finger up, orchestrating the words he knew by heart. 'Members shall live in ignominy. Their disgrace their own.' He took a sip of his beer before continuing. 'I know it's unlikely, but we can't induct someone unless we know what they did was unique.'

'Sure. Fine. But I don't think they had webcams back in the day. And besides, doesn't that mean one day we'll run out of Members?'

'You'd be surprised,' Horace said. 'Innovation of humiliation seems to be a subconscious skill of our profession.'

A laugh rippled around the room at that.

William found himself a seat next to Jessica and Susie and perused the records. Zachary had a point, it occurred to him.

Guy Fawkes and his thirty-six barrels of gunpowder was the start. The record showed him as a fanatic trying to upend British politics, but only the Right Members Club knew the truth: he had succeeded in preserving it. The assassination and scorched-earth plan had been real, but the warning letter, the capture and the disgrace were the sacrifice that protected the country. From that came the first Members, who took their sins as titles rather than shame: Pride, Greed, Wrath, Envy, Lust, Gluttony and Sloth, exiled from respectability yet devoted to the quiet preservation of Britain. Disgraced servants of the public good, working in the shadows to ensure the country survived its rulers.

The Omnibar quietened as the Members drifted off, some to their quarters, others into the night, off to tinker, bribe or black-mail in the name of national calm. Britain needed to remain dull in order for it to survive. That started and ended with politics.

Only Jessica lingered, half-drunk and restless. William's unflappable number two. She rose, stretched and paused in the doorway, her jaw set somewhere between loyalty and intrigue.

'We'll follow you until the end, William. But if we can't touch Pierce, if every trick in the book slides off him—what makes you think this Fallow idiot can help?'

William leaned back in his chair, eyes tracing the haggard wooden beams of the ceiling. 'I delayed; I was too cautious. I let his rhetoric get a foothold. Traditional methods have failed us. Pierce is a new strain, immune to the usual medicine. A modern, damn-right, futuristic "Leader". We need someone with an edge, an obscene dimension that we can't even reckon with. Fallow is perfect.'

Jessica looked at him, holding the envelope now. 'If you're sure.'

'I am. Deliver it.'

Her nod was tight, and the door seemed to slam a little heavier.

William was all alone. The dregs of amber in his glass caught the light as he raised it.

'To Mark Fallow, Member for Lust.'

9

t was the third jogger that morning that underlined the excruciating pain the Fallows were living through. Presumably on pace for a solid 5k, they'd stop and gawp. Slow down to a shuffle before the penny dropped. It was the same with the postman, the usual cheery 'Morning, Mr Fallow' replaced with a look better suited to a funeral.

Mark and Lucy were being treated like minor royals, those to be excommunicated. As the bulbs flashed and trays of tea were exchanged like currency outside their humble home in Briarwood, any hope they had of this blowing over dissipated.

Renault had spent the evening before barking. An action plan drawn up in the war room was delivered like a general on the battlefield. In truth, Mark was already in retreat. The idea of salvage felt folly; he didn't see how he could come back from this. But still, wanting to prove the good little soldier, he acquiesced to every request.

'Lucy must be there with you. Without her, it does even more harm.'

Mark winced at the fact it wasn't a question. Lucy obliged, not breaking a sweat. But deep down he felt awful about parading her as material qualification for why, in these circumstances, public masturbation wasn't so bad.

I'm married, remember! Look at my pretty wife!

Mark had tried once and once only to broach the topic of his continued career. Renault had dismissed it with one word and one look. 'Later.' Lucy tried her best to cajole, to brighten, but Mark felt himself lapsing back to a dark time, back to the days after that flight to Belfast.

His defence mechanism, his road to recovery, had been built on the idea that these horrific lurid scenarios couldn't and wouldn't come true. But now this had.

The statement was cookie-cutter. Contrite and admissive with just the right amount of wallow. Mark Wallow. A better name, he found himself thinking that morning as he got ready.

As he read, the words sounded alien. Like cotton wrapped around his tongue.

'What happened was a moment of personal misjudgement in what had been a particularly stressful day. I stress it was not intentional, it was not performative, and it was certainly not a statement on my party's politics.

'I will be conducting a full investigation into how the privacy of my own home was ruptured, and I ask for that same privacy now as I take some time to reflect and learn with my loving wife—to whom I again apologise unreservedly.'

Renault had negotiated a Q&A with the media in return for decent coverage from the big hitters. He couldn't control the questions asked but had preached common sense to the Fallows.

'What Mark did is quite cut and dried. There's a right and a wrong way to answer,' he had said.

Mark dreaded thinking about the wrong way as the first barrage came.

'Are there marital problems, Mr Fallow?'

'Absolutely not. My wife and I are united and will face this together.'

'Lucy—were you aware of Mark's fetishes?'

'That is a deeply personal question and we are entitled to our privacy.'

'Mark, have you ever met Miss Bradshaw?'

'No, but I respect her work as an actre—actor very much.'

Each was a banana skin met with sterile placative answers. If the Fallows were to bite, then the fire would reignite. Mark and Lucy stood hand in hand, batting them away, and with each, Mark swore he felt the tension radiate through his wife. He so desperately wanted to scoop her up and shield her from his mess.

Backing away, edging towards the door, it was the last question that rocked Mark and left his head spinning.

'You've inspired an online movement, Mr Fallow! How does that feel?'

'Excuse me?'

The reporter couldn't believe his luck. Fumbling to pull his phone out of his pocket, he rammed it into Mark's hand.

#MarksMen #FallowFellas pockmarked post after post. Comments like *Wank for Freedom! Mark is doing it for us! Jizz on the System!*

A video played further down. It was a man called Kevin, everything Mark thought an incel would look like.

'Mark saw that we're in a new age. Jackson attacks the institutions; Mark stands up for the downtrodden. He's our "I have a dream" moment—big media, big corporations silenced and confronted with a man's natural vigour. Jackson should consider him for deputy, I think.'

Mark wanted to scream but managed to find some poise.

'What I did was ridiculous and in no way should anyone support it. No further comment.'

It was fresh embarrassment all over again, and Mark had to fight every sinew in his body to not slam the door shut.

Back inside, he let some rage out. 'Fuck's sake. How did I not know that?' Mark started swiping through his phone. Sure enough there were dozens of messages, and social media posts all about the man that some now heralded as a hero.

'Look at this one. "Mark Fallow is the only honest politician." Because I did that? How is that honest? I'm lucky to not be on the sex offender's register—turning up every day with the codgers collecting their pensions to have my name called.'

'I don't think that's how it works, Mark.'

It was like a dam had burst. Mark stood and read more out.

'A symbol to others like us who have been marginalised and ostracised for simply being men. Alison and Dermot are unwatchable. Mark's two minutes were instantly the best thing on daytime TV.'

'Renault said they think you're their prophet,' Lucy said, her chin resting on her hands.

'You knew?'

'He called me late last night. We thought it best not to draw your attention to it. But sooner or later you'd see it on socials.'

'You spoke to Renault? Christ. Okay, so it was best to be confronted by the wolves out there, was it?' Mark said, pacing in their living room as he spiralled. 'I don't want to be their messiah.'

'Yeah, cos you're a very naughty boy,' Lucy said with a warm smile. Mark wanted to enjoy the joke but just couldn't. Instead, he scowled and turned away.

'What the fuck is this?' he said a few moments later.

'What?' Lucy was up at his side now. Her eyes widened as Mark's jaw felt primed to fall off completely.

'Offers.' He looked at her now and pointed at the screen. 'Podcast offers.'

Every man and his dog had a podcast nowadays. Maybe even the pooch that felled Lypton did. A microphone and something to say were the only prerequisites. Perhaps not even the latter.

We represent a media firm that produces high-quality commercial podcasts. We would love to explore a collab with you, Mr Fallow. Potential names and concepts below:

Male Mindset with Mark

Sticky Protest with the Fallows

Boys will be boys with Mark Fallow

There were even sponsorship ideas touted: teeth whitening, VPNs and even a webcam brand. The incredulity of it all was palpable. Mark felt as if his own teeth were going to fall out with the indignation.

'Absolutely not,' Mark repeated over and over.

'This is proof that shame is just another product,' Lucy commented.

The pair retreated to the sofa with a cup of tea and sat in silence for a long time. Not stilted awkward silence, but in a loving mending vacuum. There was nothing Mark could think to say that would be a better tonic than gripping Lucy's hand.

His future, or lack of it, flashed before his eyes. An existence predicated on a choice between shame and disgust or being paraded on panel shows. All the while his ideas for Briarwood and mental health reform would fall by the wayside.

It's good to talk. But Mark couldn't even follow his own advice. Instead just tug one out, mate, whenever you feel like it. Therapy is for chumps.

It was a little after midday when Mark's phone buzzed again. He stared at the display, fully expecting to see Renault. It wasn't. Unknown Number. In a way, Mark knew exactly where the call was coming from.

'Mr Fallow?' The woman's voice was neutral.

'Speaking.'

'This is Tara Kent. I'm calling on behalf of Jackson. Our Leader needs to see you.'

Mark shot a look at Lucy. She clasped her hands together and nodded.

'Okay, sure. When?'

'Tomorrow morning. Nine a.m. There will be a car.'

The call ended and the pair sat in silence again. This time it was different, an almost physicality to the fear and worry in the air.

'Text Renault,' Lucy said.

'He's your best mate now, is he?' Mark said, regretting his tone. He held a hand up instinctively.

> Jackson wants to see me tomorrow. What do I do?

The usual rapidity from Renault was gone. The message sat unread.

'Jackson's going to hear you out,' Lucy said. 'Surely. So we need to prep it. If he was just going to sack you, he wouldn't summon you. Renault would do the firing. We can rescue this; we can pivot. It's just a lesson in spin, and one you get very early into your career.'

Mark loved her. The optimism was almost infectious. Almost.

Deep down in the pit of his stomach, Mark only felt dread.

He felt out of his depth, out of control and out of time.

YOU ARE NOT ALONE

Breaking News: Mark Fallow, Member for Briarwood caught with his trousers down—genius or scandal for the Pierce Promise? How will Jackson respond?

10

Under different circumstances Mark would have been excited to be standing where he was.

The famous door was an impressive specimen, bigger and shinier than he had thought. No sign of Larry yet, but perhaps Jackson wasn't a cat person and Larry had been whisked off by the intelligence services.

The car had arrived exactly when Tara had said it would, nine o'clock sharp. A further message had come through an hour earlier that morning. 'Stop whatever you're doing when it arrives.'

Stopping what Mark was doing would have been fine advice two days ago.

As he waited alone in the seat of power, he felt anything but. Instead, he ruminated on a question he had tried to answer his whole adult life: 'Am I a good person?'

Lucy had helped him get better; life was good, then he'd had a wank and the walls fell in around him. His mind ran away with thoughts that threatened to paralyse him. He took a breath.

Focus on what you're saying to Jackson when he walks through that door, Mark.

He'd only been an MP for a week. There was so much he wanted to do. He needed to keep that front and centre. If Mark was an MP, he could help people. He could make it so people like him didn't have to suffer in silence. Maybe if he could convince Jackson of his passion, he could survive this. A second chance, that was all he wanted.

The door opened, and in walked the man that had dominated Mark's life for the past year.

Jackson took one look and formed his first impression of the wanker standing in front of him.

'Mark, good to see you. Thanks for coming.'

'Mr Pierce, sir.'

Mark filled the silence as words tumbled from him. 'Let me start by saying how much I believe in what you're doing. What we're doing. The mission. Politics needs you; we need you. Being elected was such an honour—an honour only possible because of you.'

He wasn't stopping. 'I made a mistake. There is no excuse for it. Only context. Oxytocin, serotonin, and endocannabinoids. Chemicals—it's chemical and natural. It was a stressful morning and I was alone in the house. It wasn't even proper porn. I'm so ashamed. If you see fit to keep me onboard, I will repay you and be forever in your debt. I have plans on how to help my constituency, and I would like a chance. Well, a second chance. To try and deliver for them.'

'We think you're a future star, Mark. I've been following your career with great interest. Your crusade for simple and accessible mental health support is exactly the sort of policy I would want. Sit down, Mark. Look, we can figure this out. Would you like a drink? A coffee? Or something stronger?'

'That's great to hear. Yes, a coffee would be lovely, please.'

Jackson pressed his intercom button. 'Tara, a coffee.'

It was about fifteen seconds from buzzer to the coffee being with Mark.

'Where were we? Oh yes, your incident. Look, Mark, you aren't the first, and you won't be the last MP to make a fool of himself in front of the public. It's in their DNA. At some point they will screw up and it will have to be dealt with. Fortunately for you, I have the largest mandate ever commanded, so I can do exactly as I please.'

'Yes, exactly. It wasn't illegal; it wasn't even particularly graphic. Like, you didn't see any of the, erm, finished product.'

'So I could wave all this away. I could tell the country that it was a human mistake. We could promote your agenda for mental health. Spin it as a man with his own demons battling back to take control. Changing for the better, overcoming adversity. That would play well, I think.'

Of course Jackson understood. Of course Jackson would make it right. The relief was immense. 'Wonderful. That's a brilliant plan. I knew you'd be able to help.' Mark's voice broke slightly as a wave of gratitude overwhelmed him.

Jackson looked down at his phone. The text instruction, clear.

We will use Fallow as the figurehead.

Jackson looked up. 'Help . . . yes, help. That's a good word, isn't it? If we did that, if I did that, who would it help? You, certainly. But me? No. Who helps me, Mark?'

'I will, Mr Pierce. You will not have another MP that works as hard as me.'

'Call me Jackson, Mark. We're all friends here. We help our friends, don't we? You said it yourself, you're fully invested in the mission, in what we're doing here.'

'Of course.' Mark sipped his coffee, starting to relax.

'We could look at this another way.'

Mark nodded and murmured assent.

'The mission is to do away with the old norms. The old way of doing things. Complacency, nepotism, scratching backs for scratching backs' sake has crept into every facet of this system.

I'm making good progress so far, but every engine needs fuel. Every cause needs a martyr.' The last sentence curled out of Jackson's lips like a dagger.

Mark jerked into mild panic. 'I'm happy to go on TV again and publicly apologise. I already spoke to my wife about attending some counselling. I can donate to charities too.' Mark was starting to grovel. 'Whatever we need to do to get back on task.'

Jackson smiled as he spoke. 'When I was a child, I didn't have a home. I didn't have parents. I barely had a sense of myself. I thought I was sick. Infected with something that made the world around me reject my very presence.'

'Sorry to hear—'

Jackson cut him off. 'I don't tell you this to elicit sympathy. I don't need sympathy. You see, I realised in time that it wasn't I who was infected. It was the rest of the world. As soon as I accepted that fact, I started to win. The state makes men, the system makes sheep. Do you understand me, Mark?'

'Yes, of course.' He hadn't a clue but thought it best to agree.

'I doubt you do. I sometimes don't. But realise this: you're helping me to achieve something greater than any of this. The country chose me as someone who is going to do what he says. I want the old ways gone, and so do you. You're part of my team. How do you think I'm going to look if within my first week one of my MPs is pleasuring himself to some old tart and gets to carry on with little more than a soapy apology?'

Jackson answered his own question. 'It will make me look weak, Mark. You don't want me to look weak, do you, Mark? No, good man, I can see you shaking your head, so we are in agreement, then.'

'Agreement, sir?' Mark jabbered.

At that point the world shuddered into slow motion for Mark. Into the room stepped Renault.

'Mr Fallow, we need you to sign this.' He passed a letter to Mark.

It was a fully prepared resignation letter. He scanned it, his eyes in disbelief at what they read.

. . . I have let my wife down, my constituents down, and Jackson down . . .

. . . I am not a symbol of anything other than the corruption of politics . . .

. . . I have a deep-seated neurological addiction to pornography . . .

. . . I believe in our Leader; I should resign immediately . . .

The thought bounced around his head—*it wasn't even proper porn*—a ridiculous statement but alas, all that his brain could muster.

Jackson closed the meeting with a final remark.

'You're young. You're like those men who idolise you: foolish and lost. Lost without purpose. You'll see this as a kindness in the years to come. Deep down you didn't want to be an MP. Who would? You'll find something else, and believe me, whatever you thought you were going to do, whatever you thought you were going to achieve in my government, it would have paled into insignificance compared to how I can use your resignation to further the Pierce Promise. Thank you for your service, if a week counts as service. Now fuck off, you wanker.' Jackson laughed aloud.

Renault pulled Mark up from his seat with one tug and walked him out of the office. He ensured Mark signed the document before having him escorted out to a waiting car that took him straight home, not before giving him a fun fact for the ride home.

At just over seven days, excluding deaths, Mark Fallow was the shortest-serving MP in history.

11

Mark was adrift. Whatever the Prime Minister—sorry, the Leader—the country or the Right Members Club were planning or whispering about him, it no longer mattered.

'I'm off, love.' Lucy poked her head round the living room door.

'Mmm.'

'This Workforce Growth Bill is scary. Jackson's got the country looking the other way. Jane is chomping at the bit.' She had stepped inside now. Mark didn't bother to look up.

Lucy took the hint, giving Mark a warm kiss on his forehead and departing.

She was a saint, but even she had to return to the real world. Work called, and believe it or not, a solitary week of being an MP does not a rich boy make. Their pre-election budgeting had been vigorous. Mark's modest savings from his middling software sales job would tide them over until his parliamentary salary arrived. Combined with Lucy's steady but unremarkable income as an accountant for the local builders' merchants, it meant the Fallows got their own small appetiser of the cost-of-living crisis, a nibble compared to what others endured but a taste all the same.

Mark's mind was stuck on food, it seemed, as he watched a repeat of an old *MasterChef*. Gregg Wallace licked his lips over some sort of meat, whilst Marcus Wareing referred to everything on the plate as cookery. It cut to a talking head with one of the contestants.

'My food is modern, with a nod to the past. It's conventional comfort and unique innovation.'

'Fuck off, mate. It's a duck breast.' Mark was a fair few beers deep and afraid of considering his future.

He was afraid of everything, in fact. The result of having been turned into national policy.

Jackson was a breath of fresh air for many: opportunistic, ruthless and calculating, but most importantly, he did what he said he would. He had looked Mark up and down, fondled him like a widget at B&Q and declared: *He'll do. Stick him in my basket.*

It was a painful realisation that the newspaper headlines had already been set before Mark had even sat down at No. 10 that morning.

CRUSADE: PIERCE'S NEW PROMISE

The scandal was a godsend, arriving at a perfect time just as Jackson was meeting resistance to dismantling the House of Lords. He seized the moment, sacrificing Mark to advance his agenda. Mark was painted as a creep, a man with a fetish for older women, emblematic of everything wrong with a morally bankrupt political class. In Parliament, Jackson quipped that Members couldn't be trusted to vote responsibly if they couldn't be trusted to use a webcam. Jackson's response was almost hypnotic in its precision. Despite the scandal involving his own party's MP, his swift and decisive action earned him praise. Here was a leader who claimed the old ways were broken, and when one of his own confirmed it, he cauterized the wound and made the scandal a rallying cry.

Jackson introduced sweeping reforms under the guise of

restoring public trust: term limits for MPs, redrawn constituency maps to reduce their numbers and, most prominently, the introduction of a Leader's Executive Order.

Overnight the national debate was reshaped. Class, culture wars, immigration and the economy took a backseat to a simple idea: integrity. Mark was the petri dish in which the argument could flourish. Immediately the cult-like buzz that formed around the Fallow Incident was like the Christmas lights switch-on.

Here, look, these sorts of men worship disgrace. Do we want that anywhere near our politics?

The answer was a resounding no.

And it wasn't just Westminster. Integrity was mooted as an addition to the national curriculum. The BBC trialled a companion show to *The Moral Maze* entitled *Ethics Hour*, where a cavalcade of talking heads and celebrities would get together and examine each other's indiscretions. Heartfelt, teary, impassioned speeches about how close these people came to their own 'Fallow Fall'.

There were subtler changes too. Society had begun to warp as it stared back into the mirror, Jackson's reflection casting a shadow over everything. From small talk with friends and family to brazen chatter over fences and at supermarket tills, his cadence was spreading. His swagger and bluntness had rubbed off on ordinary folk.

Queues are old hat.

Council tax is antiquated.

It wasn't revolt so much as fatigue made manifest, an exhaustion with the status quo seeping into every part of daily life. Lucy had convinced Mark to brave a very not cheeky Nando's, where they had watched, stunned, as a fellow diner demanded to know why the waiter would not take their order at the table, announcing with none of Jackson's charm that they 'should take a leaf out of the Pierce Promise's playbook and bloody well adapt'.

Mark's disgrace had been repurposed into a civic virtue. He was the catalyst for change. But for Mark, buzzwords like *opportunities* and *collabs* kept coming. The larger the scandal and the bigger the fall, the more money that could be made. As the mainstream media placed integrity upon a pedestal, the counter-programming of the 'alt' became feral in its intensity. Mark had answered the door one afternoon expecting a water filter for their espresso machine. Instead he found a leech. An assistant to a producer, the gum stuck to the sole of a boot, who had memorised an elevator pitch which started the second the door had opened a crack. 'We've mapped out a H1 plan. *Celebrity Big Brother* in six months, and after that the world's your oyster.'

Mark didn't want oysters. A return to his former career of software sales was the safe choice. He'd just switch off his ambition, numb himself to everything and make peace that this was his punishment. He had Lucy still, so that would be his joy; everything else was tainted.

He wasn't sure if he hated Jackson or if deep down he was disappointed he didn't hate him as much as he should have. Wanting to be liked was a curse, not even allowing Mark to feel rage in the correct way.

A churlish, half-cut voice spoke to him.

What if you can use these media opportunities as a platform? To champion mental health and spin the narrative to suit.

Then he was interrupted, the dark side, the obsessional side.

You're as likely to do it again. Sick fuck.

So paralysis won. The antidote to an overwhelming need for control was to do nothing. Mark would lose, of course, but the thoughts wouldn't win.

Mark had learned his lesson. He should have learned it after his first foray into politics. Not this second botched attempt. He thought back to his political internship at university. Six weeks with Frank Hower, MP for Luton North, working on local charity initiatives. It had lit a small fire in Mark; it felt important. Nearly every night that summer, he would meet up with Lucy at the Red Lion in Holborn. There was an ironic beauty to discussing economic reform whilst living off 2-4-1 drinks at the bar. But in his final week, Frank shattered the illusion with an offhand remark: 'I can't pay you a living wage; maybe in a few years.' There was no money in politics unless you were born into it.

Lucy's offer to support him if he pursued politics crushed him as much as it made him love her. He couldn't let her do it. Dreams didn't pay rent, and he wasn't about to become a burden. By graduation, Lucy had her future locked in and Mark had to pivot. Software sales wasn't the dream. 'Just for a year or two,' he'd said. Ten years later, on a sales call, he'd boarded that flight in Belfast.

He resolved to lie there until Lucy got home, as usual. Or at least he would have if the distinct sound of the letterbox hadn't echoed in the hallway.

He raised a hand and pointed at the cat. 'Go get it, Chunk.'

Chunk refused, because he was a cat. Mark hoisted himself up and tottered out of the living room and over to the front door.

Sitting on the doormat was a small off-white envelope. Quite unremarkable. Except as Mark picked it up he noticed a deep purple wax seal on the back. There was an image stamped into it. It was a hat, one of those old style buckled hats. Long like a stovepipe, tapering at the top.

Inside was a stiff card, embroidered around the edges with purple stitching and embossed lettering. Two sentences stared back at Mark.

You are not alone. Meet with us
George & Dragon, Lambeth, Next Friday

Mark put the letter down on the side and went back to the sofa.

I'm not becoming a fucking influencer.

12

'Esther Murphy died because of men like Mark Fallow.' Jackson repeated the line in a few different ways in front of the mirror that morning.

It was bold, brash and to the point. The louder the message, the greater the reach.

A little after breakfast he'd summoned Tara to the cabinet room in 10 Downing Street.

'Remove the chairs. Make them stand.'

'For the reshuffle?' she'd asked.

Jackson gave her a look. She nodded; diligence and discretion were personality traits for her. But Jackson wasn't finished. He swirled a finger and asked, 'Tara, tell me, have you ever been to IKEA?'

'Yes. Good meatballs.'

'I've heard. But what do you make of the flat-pack furniture?'

Tara flattened her pencil skirt down, as if the question had creased it. 'It's infuriating. But serves a purpose to a point.'

'Quite. Cheap, disposable and ultimately ending in disassembly.' Jackson thumped the table. 'Then I want this taken apart too.'

'Of course, Jackson.'

The media were bemused Jackson was readying a reshuffle this early. Bemused and plainly wrong. Jackson planned to permanently dismantle his Cabinet that morning—less work than assembling your average bookcase too.

His ministers turned up at 10 Downing Street like lambs to the slaughter. Herded into the room without chairs, a table toppled on its side, legs splayed across the floor. If they hadn't seen it coming by now, they were as dumb as Jackson suspected; if they had, then they were too cowardly to do anything about it.

'What's all this about, Jackson? A practical joke?' the Transport Secretary dared.

The cabinet room was a symbol of the old ways. Now it truly offered nothing. No comfort, no purpose and no function. Even the snacks and coffee had vanished. Jackson let the silence linger for a moment before pointing to the wall.

'Screens. And then there, where the table was, sofas.' He turned on the spot, pointed to the far wall. 'Maybe a pinball machine too, a callback, retro, like you.'

He surveyed them now, this sorry lot. Their dour suits and wiry hair framing coffee-stained teeth as they practised that insincere smile that politicians do. Turning his attention to one in particular, he began the cull.

'We're going in a different direction; you will no longer be needed.'

'Sorry, Jackson, what does that mean?' his Foreign Secretary asked.

'It means that I don't know how you can help. I don't know what you do.'

'I'm the Foreign Secretary— '

'That's just a fucking job title, Keith.'

Jackson looked around the room. All of their heads were bobbing. Like chickens in a coop debating how much feed they could stuff in their beaks before they were carted off to slaughter. Too late, now there was a wolf in the hen house.

Keith puffed his cheeks, stamped his feet. 'What are you going to do, replace us all at once?'

'No, actually.'

'How will you run the country?'

'Like I've been doing. You must see you've been nothing more than a holdover. I couldn't sweep everything away instantly. I needed a bigger broom.'

'I don't understand. You're a . . . you're nothing but a rabble-rouser,' Keith stammered, others murmuring, their bobbing increasing.

Jackson stood firm. 'Your words cut like a plastic spork, Keith. You think I don't have a rational argument? You're out of touch. My argument is the *most* rational. The civil servants, the real folk, do all the work, or whatever it is your departments actually get through. I'll just cut the middlemen out now and continue on.'

Another dreadful man spoke, Thomas, the Chancellor of the Exchequer. 'I know we're breaking new ground here, Jackson, but this is too far, even for you.'

'It's not far enough in my opinion, and long overdue.'

He turned his attention back to Keith. 'Besides, we are clamping down on corruption, aren't we? How will the public look upon a Foreign Secretary with a Russian mistress?'

'What? How—'

'This is a much-needed reform. You'll realise in time. Your cars are waiting for you outside. Thank you for your service.'

'You can't do this. We'll defect. Fight you.'

Jackson laughed. One hand slipped into his pocket.

'Esther Murphy died because of men like Mark Fallow. Men like you. I have to deliver on my promises. You can fight me, but with what support?'

Since that rather fortunate business with Fallow, Jackson had acquired a taste for political leverage. The ruthless effectiveness of offering one of your own up as an inadequacy delivered resounding results.

He ran his campaign on the promise of burning away the

decay, and his public approval soared as he started the procedure in his own back garden. Using the Fallow Incident as a pilot, Jackson appeared on *Politics Live*. His old chum Katie Turner was delighted with the ratings, or at least she should be. Jackson declared that Britain was in a *National Crisis of Morality*, following it up with a swift appearance in the Commons the next day; he transferred himself further executive powers to govern as he saw fit.

Any and every slight digression by an MP piled onto the stack of evidence for Jackson to tout to the public. While some had legitimately done wrong (expense fraud, violent altercations, sexual misdemeanours), others were strung up and summarily dismissed by the most vicious adjudicator of all: the public.

Renault had called in favours. Cashed in political capital. Weeded out the critical information when it mattered most. He was not discerning when it came to the grey areas of people's lives. Recreational drug use, driving on one drink, even failing to deliver on constituency surgery promises were enough for Jackson to focus the microscope.

All in all, in the month after Fallow's fall, Jackson shed seventeen MPs with no formal dates set for by-elections. Jackson argued passionately that Britain was evidently in ethical decay and needed immediate remedial work to buttress the foundations. The traditional mechanisms of electoral norms could wait while he got the 'builders in'.

The dissolution of the House of Lords was hastened, made possible by the fuel Fallow's sacrifice injected into Jackson's rage engine. The Opposition, what there was of it, managed to band together a small clump of dissenters that blocked his progress initially through the medieval wizardry of parliamentary statutes and customs, but the stronger Jackson's cries of crisis were, the quicker they proved to be unwound.

Without the Lords, his newly self-appointed executive powers allowed him to spill into the vacuum created by a non-codified constitution. Madam Speaker and her cronies tried to block the way with liberal use of litigation, but it was all too slow, all too obvious. Of course, the Prime Minister could not simply appoint judges. Not yet, anyway. But a few choice introductions, favours called in at the right dinners, and quiet assurances passed through hands that never appeared on any record provided judiciary lubricant, which meant Jackson had everything he needed to sidestep, dodge, and carry on as if going for a stroll on a summer's day. Sometimes his phone even buzzed with advice before he had thought to ask for it. Considering the heft of history he was pulling against, he was making great progress, but he could always go faster.

The Pierce£ went from strength to strength, until it didn't. But that was what crypto did. Boom then slump. It would come again and again. The smart people made money, the dumb learned a lesson.

Business was happy with his Workforce Growth Bill, and every single train journey in the morning would offer a bacon roll to its passengers owing to the Fast-Track Food Production Scheme.

Even the motion to abolish speed limits across the country was picking up pace. The public was in love, or so the polls said. Life moved so quickly that as long as people felt something was good, they didn't look too far into it. This eschewing of detail was the political kindling from which Jackson's fire raged.

Of course some pointed out that paying for voter loyalty and hampering the human rights of non-UK nationals was outrageous. Speed limits—it was argued—were there for public safety. Only the subsect of dissenters who were vegetarian or vegan found something to moan about with the train policy. People enjoyed bacon. Who knew?

Jackson strode into the Chamber of the House of Commons, poised to speak to the nation. The Speaker was still there, Rachel Jenkins. He allowed her to remain in a modified role akin to a producer on a TV show, cajoling the audience of the background extras of MPs as Jackson made his remarks.

'Ladies and gentlemen of the British public, today I announce the next step on the road to delivering the Pierce Promise. This morning I have streamlined the decision-making process in government, consolidating power where before it was disparate, spread too far and too wide.'

A check of his phone:

Make it clear nothing changes for the public.

'That Ministers would presume in-depth knowledge about the departments they were thrust into. Nonsense! For I must reveal the truth. The truth is that the real knowledge comes from the regular men and women in these departments.'

He was enjoying the way the words were falling today.

'The experts, the veterans, the people who have been living and breathing their respective professions for years, for decades. I will now receive their reports, their data, and tackle the problems and meet the opportunities of Britain in one joined-up motion.'

Rachel offered him a weak smile.

Remember: minimal interference, maximum freedom. We need them ready for what comes next.

'Rest assured, every decision that will come from this government will come from me and me alone. You are free to get on with your lives as you see fit. Minimal interference, maximum freedom. Thank you, Britain.'

Walking back through the Chamber, he basked in the

Speaker's directed applause. Another step toward the goal. Another piece of the puzzle completed.

Jackson checked social media. Trending right at the top: #TheBenevolentDictator.

INDUCTION

Breaking News: House of Lords dissolution bill passes 498 to 97 with 55 abstentions—Jackson Pierce uses executive powers to enforce from next week

13

Mark didn't even bother to tell Lucy. The letterbox clanged again late last night; another envelope, another card through the door. The fifth one in a month, but this one was different.

Pierce isn't what he seems. Mark, you're the key.

For a man who worried about acting on the insane, Mark jumped in again without thinking. Perhaps when you've been to the bottom and rolled around in shit for so long that you've developed a crust, a risk didn't seem like such a bad thing.

In front of him lay the George & Dragon pub in Lambeth, an abandoned boarded-up shitheap, and a massive shitheap at that. Mark idled on the pavement for so long that he was bumped into by a pedestrian. A cheery-sounding Yorkshire accent burst from the man.

'Do pardon me, son.'

Mark stepped to the left, mumbling his response. 'Sorry, mate, not with it today.'

The stranger nodded and walked on.

This was a washout, a prank, a waste of his time. Mark had seen a *Greggs* near the tube station back down the road. Time for a sausage roll and a solemn ride back to the dreaded office. He was grateful for employment back at the software company, but the novelty of fielding questions on his departure from politics had faded about five seconds into his first team meeting. He didn't blame them; it wasn't every day you got to work with a political movement.

But didn't you see the webcam was on?

Why Jill Bradshaw?

What's Jackson Pierce like?

Mark drove his hands deep into his pockets. He froze in his tracks. There was something in the left one. Something that had not been there before. An envelope, much like the ones he had been receiving. It was new, unopened. The familiar wax seal with the stovepipe hat.

Fumbling it open, there was a new card, this time with a new message.

Down the alley. Look for RMC.

He scanned around him. Against his better judgement, he headed back to the old pub and aimed up the alley. Sure enough, there was a shabby door with *RMC*, so faint, in fact, if you weren't thinking about those letters you wouldn't notice it. He turned the handle and entered.

Mark stood in astonishment.

It was like a rabbit warren, like a TARDIS. He had two corridors arcing to his left and right. To the right there were bar stools, booths and a fruit machine. This section was done up to resemble something from the eighties, or at least what he knew of the Queen Vic on *EastEnders*.

If he looked the other way, he could see another style of bar. This was more like a tavern. Like something from the olden days. It wouldn't have surprised him to see some hay on the floor, a gunslinger at the bar and a horse in the corner. Flanking the corridors were portraits with plaques but no names. Beautifully painted men and women. A simple title and date underneath: *Member for Envy 1943–1986, Member for Sloth 1976–1998.*

Mark saw a staircase that was hidden behind some tables in the corner. Approaching the bottom of the stairs, he could swear he heard faint chatting alongside music. Classical music.

He crept up the stairs, trying to limit his breathing so he could listen harder. The voices were getting louder. There was a door at the top. Just before he turned the handle, he noticed another painting to his left. Mark was floored. He almost let go of the railing and hurtled back down the stairs. Steadying himself, he leant closer to the picture.

'It's me. Why is it me?' Half under his breath.

It was a dashing painting of Mark, but instead of his name it was labelled *Member for Lust*—with a space to finish the date.

In his stupor he bumped sideways against the wall. The voices stopped. *Shit.* Snared by an overwhelming sense of dread, Mark had no choice but to confront whoever was coming through that door. The footsteps got closer.

The door opened.

'Mark, good to see you! Welcome! Come in, come in; we have a lot of work to do.' And with that, the big Yorkshireman who'd bumped into him earlier embraced Mark and pulled him into the room.

Mark's mind was flying.

What the fuck is going on? The guy from outside . . . am I being kidnapped? Getting murdered, great. Six of them. Maybe a sex thing? They liked my video . . . am I going to be sodomised in Lambeth on a work day? Wait, is that food? Music? A party? Someone's birthday? There's no cake.

'Mark, it's alright. We're not going to hurt you.'

The big burly Yorkshire-accented man handed him a flagon. Without thinking, Mark took a sip. *Idiot! Drugged!*

'William,' the man said, pulling off his glove and offering a clammy handshake. 'Nice to meet you properly. We've got quiche, too.'

'Where am I? What kind of quiche?' Mark asked.

Next to speak was an older gentleman, a well-dressed black

man with wild hair. 'Mr Fallow, sir, it's an honour. Horace Knight, Member for Greed.'

'A bit early with the titles, Horace; Mark's acclimating here.' William laughed.

'Mark, I'm Jessica Campbell. Those envelopes? That was me.' A woman with long red hair.

Mark was trying to stay in the moment. It was difficult as more people spoke. Trying to keep his wits about him while being polite and remembering his potential kidnappers' names.

'Wait, Jessica Campbell? I know you.'

She nodded, looking at William. 'Later, later,' he said.

Another face he thought he recognised. 'Mark, this is Zachary Grim.' William introduced the man who leant against the bar, disinterested.

Two for two in terms of recognition. Like a roulette wheel, Mark was spun again, and this time he was in front of a younger woman.

'Mr Fallow, I've heard so much about you. Terrible shame about your video. I'm Susie, Susie Shiq.' A smaller woman with a warm smile.

Mark blushed. Of course they knew about Wankgate.

'And last but by no means least, this is the formidable Derek Strong,' William declared.

Strong was short. Where Mark was oblong and spread out, this man was square and condensed. He clasped Mark's hand with a grip like a vice and spoke in a Geordie accent.

'Hullo there, Mark. Don't worry, I like Jill Bradshaw too.'

William gestured for everyone to quieten.

'Mark, I'm sorry; this must feel like a lot. But we've got you here finally, and things are moving quickly. We need you onboard.'

'What is this place? Why do I recognise some of you?'

'It's a long story,' Jessica said, and she turned to William. 'Maybe if we explained properly?'

'Fine, I'll give him the headlines now.' William took a sharp intake of breath and began.

'This is the Right Members Club. All of us are disgraced MPs. We work behind the scenes to prevent crises that could destabilise the country. We've been doing this since 1605—since Guy Fawkes, actually. We are the guardians of continuity in Britain.'

Mark could have asked any one of about a million questions at that point. He took his time while his mind exploded like every firework show ever all at one. These six strangers, who were somehow familiar, stared at him.

Disgraced MPs. What does that have to do with guarding Britain?

Mark settled on his question. It was in two parts.

'Okay. Right. Firstly, you mean the bonfire night Guy? As in gunpowder, treason and plot? And secondly, do you have a toilet I could use, please?'

William laughed and pointed across the room.

Mark needed to be comfortable. He felt like he was going to be here a while.

14

Mark fidgeted on his bar stool, cutlery clinking on the plate as he finished his quiche. It was tame, as far as quiches went, with a soggy crust and mild burst of cheddar.

'Jessica. Perhaps Mark would feel at ease if he understood he's not alone,' William said.

She sighed, topped up her wine glass and started to speak. 'I used to run eight surgeries a month down in Devon. Meeting people, helping them where I could. It was addictive, but the more I helped, the ambition grew.

'I convinced myself that if I could get a seat in the Cabinet, I could help my community more. So I spent more time in London, and my second home became my first priority. My constituents resented the gap I left. I don't blame them now. I was angry at the time. That was my mindset when I sent those emails.'

Mark made a noise of recognition. Her emails had been leaked to the press. They derided her Devon constituents, calling them *Cabbage Patch Folk*. Declaring that if they had even just half the culture and intelligence of Londoners then they would be able to grasp how she was doing all this to help them.

'I wrote the emails, I can't deny that. I spent a lot of time angry at the fact they were leaked. I've come to realise that it was for the best. It wasn't long before I fell on my sword, left the job that I loved and the people I once put upon a pedestal.

What do they say? Pride comes before a fall? Well, that's me, the Member for Pride.'

'I'm really sorry, Jessica,' Mark said.

'Don't be. I've made peace with it.'

'What's with the seven deadly sins? You said you were—what, Greed, Horace? And Jessica, you're Pride?'

Jessica welcomed the change in topic. 'Members are named after the seven deadly sins. A parody of tradition. Our founders thought no better mantles existed than that of sin.'

'There can only ever be seven,' Horace added.

'I'm Pride, Horace is Greed, Derek Sloth, Susie Envy, Zachary represents Gluttony, and you'll be Lust,' Jessica said.

Mark looked at William. 'And you?'

'I'm Wrath.'

'Blimey,' Mark said, finishing his second slice of quiche.

William cleared his throat and shifted focus. 'We've been trying to rein Jackson in.'

Before William could continue, Jessica spoke. 'While we exist to protect, we don't want to interfere too heavily. Carmichael was a special case.'

Mark felt William's eyes on him. 'Carmichael? That was you?'

'We intervene when there's a threat to continuity. She would have caused unrest, violence and untold atrocities if allowed to continue.' Jessica said it with a slight waver to her voice.

'Jackson's a threat to continuity,' Mark said.

'Perhaps,' Susie said, 'but he's united everyone against politicians, not the country.'

Zachary grunted from the bar. 'For now, the people are being lied to.'

William nodded. 'We didn't know then; we do now.'

'Lied to? Your invitation said he's not what he seems. All you mean is you dislike the fact he won. Fair and square, I should add,' Mark said, a prickle of indignation surprising him.

A quieter, more solemn voice spoke: Derek's. 'Esther Murphy.' He stepped forward. 'I went there, Mark. I have contacts. It was foul play, but it was covered up.'

Mark blinked. 'Murdered? By Jackson?'

William waved a hand. 'The timing was too perfect.'

Mark felt rage swell. That was new. He shouted. *'Perfect? Someone did this to her. What are you talking about, perfect?'*

William tried to calm the tension. 'It's a tragedy. A crime. But it's sensitive; if we are to use it, we need to be certain. Otherwise we risk causing chaos. That's the burden of the Club. Consider, observe. Wait for the right moment. Then strike. We don't tell you this to upset you, Mark; we tell you this because we want to correct it.'

Jessica slid her phone to William. 'Jackson's about to speak.'

William fiddled with the phone and turned the volume up.

'A super-secret special club and we're huddling around a phone,' Zachary quipped.

'Eyes failing you, Grim?' Jessica offered in return.

According to the ticker tape, Jackson Pierce had arrived at the Commons with a special announcement to make.

'How quick could he pass it?' Susie asked.

'With the Lords gone, it would fly through . . . ' Horace trailed off.

'Have I missed something here?' Mark asked, perplexed.

William looked away for a moment as he looked at his own phone resting on his thigh as if digesting something. He turned to Mark.

'I know you're wary. I would be too. But I can prove what we're saying. We know what Jackson is about to do. We believe he's going to call a referendum and after that, call a vote for a motion of No Confidence.'

'A what? Why would he call that on himself?'

'No, not on himself. No Confidence in Parliament.'

A motion of No Confidence was something called against the Prime Minister. Against Parliament was unheard of, because it was nonsensical.

No Confidence motions were used against a premiership that was stumbling, flailing. Jackson was anything but. Mark tried to consider him using it against the Commons.

'It's the final step on his journey,' William said.

Mark scrunched his face. 'Journey to what?'

'Abolishing our way of government. Jackson would be Leader . . . indefinitely.'

'He can't do that. The constitution prevents it.'

'Jackson's using the national emergency on *morality* as a way to coerce and whip the votes.' William let the words hang for a moment. 'He'll put it to the public first as a referendum, and then use that mandate for a full motion. After that, he will suspend the next election date until such a time as he deems the crisis over.'

'How do you know this?' Mark demanded.

William flared his nostrils, certainty in his eyes. 'We've been trying to tell you! We work to stop the crisis. The constitution is unwritten but not undefended. We have people close to him —everywhere, in fact.'

Mark's frustration at the cryptic answers was building now, starting to leak from every pore like an anxious sweat. 'Not trying very hard, are you?' He addressed the whole room.

'This is why we need you. We're losing control of the situation. But I have a plan,' William added.

'What possible good can I do here?' Mark was shouting again as the emotion took hold. 'I had a wank on the internet, for fuck's sake! I am nothing, I'm no one. I have a shit job that I hate, and everyone thinks I'm a colossal twat.'

Before anyone could reply to Mark's outburst, Jackson appeared at the despatch box and began to speak.

He announced the referendum as if ordering a coffee. Light, breezy, without a care in the world. The country would vote on the concept of Parliament with a direct question about the suitability of MPs. William was proven right. Mark sat there, head spinning.

Afterwards, William's tone was quieter, more considered. He spoke only to Mark. 'What you did is exactly why I chose you to be the next Member for Lust. A disgraced MP with nothing else to lose. Do you want to stop Jackson?'

Mark took a deep breath and picked at the first question swirling in his mind.

'How exactly do seven disgraced MPs save Britain?'

William looked at his charges. The Members skirted the room.

'It's the little things, Mark,' Derek said. 'I felt the same when I joined. This is a secret club that saves the country, right? Oooooh, superheroes. We've even got a headquarters, the Omnibar. Utter nonsense.'

Mark couldn't help himself. 'Omnibar?'

Derek smiled. 'Every era of pub all in one place. The Club's been around since 1605. Back then, once you were out of the game, there wasn't much to do besides drink and scheme. The original Members met in taverns, like Mr Fawkes and his fellows. This one's the Fawkes Tavern, in fact. My favourite's from the 1920s—proper bit of glam, that.'

Zachary grunted. 'Renamed the George & Dragon in the 1950s, but it's the same spot. Each generation added their flavour. British politics runs on in-jokes; we do too.'

Mark nodded. 'The little things?'

'He's tiny, isn't he?' Zachary laughed.

'Ignore Grim. Yes, the little things. I was a big fan of delegating. Meet people, collect favours and avoid paperwork. Workshy, you could say. My downfall.'

'How so?' Mark asked.

'Francesca Blake was her name. My laziness was the reason she died.'

He paused, eyes fixed on Mark's. 'She was teaching in Libya. Wrong place, wrong time. Relations were tense after Lockerbie. I was a Junior Minister then and handled her release. Should have been simple. A few dissidents traded for her return. I delegated the paperwork. They made a pig's ear of it. Delays, mistakes. Infection doesn't care about red tape. By the time we got her home, she was beyond help. But it wasn't in the press. It would have sunk the government. Instead in our wisdom we spun it into the fact Gaddafi didn't look after his prisoners. We used it, Mark. We fucking used it as a political chip. Tell that to her family over there. Quietly, of course, I was dispatched with.'

It started to make sense. 'And you got an envelope?' Mark asked.

Derek shook his head and looked at William. 'Not at first. I don't know why. William's infinite wisdom, I guess.'

William looked down at the floor. 'You weren't ready, Derek.'

Mark considered if he was ready. What criteria had he met? He held his tongue.

'No, that's probably true. It got pretty dark for a time . . .' Derek lost his train of thought, as if remembering a page of a book that was pitch black. 'Eventually I was the Member for Sloth. I hated myself, but green shoots come from even the most scorched of earth given enough time.'

'Little things . . .' Mark reminded him.

'Yes, and you know it turns out having made so many contacts over the years, it gave me a unique position as a bit of a fixer for the club. It takes a while to get there, but a sloth sees a lot stuck up a tree, you know? That's how I found out about Esther Murphy.'

William placed his hand on Mark's shoulder. 'We use what

we did to help us correct and right the ship. Come with me. I've got something to show you.'

Full of quiche and questions, Mark slid off the stool and asked where they were going.

'We're off to see a man about some bacon.'

15

About ten minutes away from their destination, William thought it time to brief Mark. He gripped the old steering wheel of his third-generation red Ford Escort and spoke.

'You might not believe it, but right now you represent a real chance of derailing Pierce. We've gotten in his way a few times, slowed some motions, interrupted schemes, but the Members are getting . . . I'm getting frustrated we can't land a decisive blow.'

'What would decisive look like to a man like him?'

'Jackson's done a lot in a short amount of time. He's oscillated between big, like the House of Lords, and small, like the bacon rolls on trains. It's the little things, remember. Bacon is his most media-friendly policy. It's not flippant, though; it's calculated. The cryptocurrency is a slower burn, canning the cabinet was explosive—but bacon . . . near universally loved, isn't it?'

Mark nodded.

'People are strange, Mark. If they're at the supermarket, they'll consider the difference between organic and free-range eggs. Is this coffee fairtrade? Sliced white bread has become synonymous with the devil. There is a cognitive dissonance when making the decision yourself. But if you offer something for free while telling them they deserve it, they stop the cycle. They have to accept it. It's for them, it's theirs. Ever heard of the idea of the *norm of reciprocity*?'

'The what of what?'

'No, not many people have. It's some bit of dusty research from the seventies. When people receive a gift, they are more likely to comply with a future request. No matter how small the gift, no matter if the gift was unsolicited.'

Mark felt his cogs turning. 'When is a bacon sandwich not a bacon sandwich?'

'Bingo! Let's just say there's no such thing as a free lunch. Or breakfast, in this case.'

'So what exactly does he get out of it?'

'He's not stupid, is Pierce. It's a tool to get the public to accept some more of the brazen moves. Bacon today, Lords tomorrow and then move against the Commons the week after.'

Mark fidgeted at that. William continued as the car navigated a roundabout.

'All we can do as Members is work in the shadows. Back in the day, they'd be there, underneath it all. Networks, tunnels, all a bit more practical. Now we have to do things like this. Anyway, that's in the past.'

William adjusted the knobs and dials of the old car.

'We're a proud nation of temporarily frustrated millionaires. We know best, and if we're not winning then it's someone else's fault. Immigrants, older generations or the ruling elite. We don't like being told what to do, and we don't like feeling like we're missing out. Piece by piece, Jackson has tried to paint us a picture of why the sort of change he's enacting is needed, and crucially why it's helpful to us. If he presents enough *quick wins,* most people, and that's the key part'—William paused to stress the next word again—'*most* switch that part of the brain off and give him a pass for future changes.'

William turned the key; the engine faded. They were alone in the quiet car in a nondescript car park.

In front of them was a poster child for architectural depression. Prefabricated corrugated tin-roofed hovels. Boxy, rectangular tubs of buildings, with cracked beige walls and small recessed windows. It was hard to find a pretty-looking industrial estate in Britain, but this might be up there with the worst of them.

Popular after the war, when the idea was to throw as much bricks and mortar as possible at the local environment and see what stuck. This stuck, and it now stuck out like a sore thumb.

William jutted his head forward, pointing out the far building to Mark. 'Streatham Bacon Curing. One of seven new pop-up production facilities across the country. People have no clue the demand the free daily bacon cob puts on existing supply chains. Jackson saw it though, so he passed the wonderfully worded Fast-Track Food Production and Planning Exemption Scheme or the FFPPE. A genius piece of legislation, designed to cut through the usual bureaucratic red tape and expedite the creation of new food production facilities.'

'This place looks old, though.'

William nodded. 'To sweeten the deal, a neat little addendum allowed for the conversion of existing government-funded properties, should they be deemed *strategically important*.'

Inside they found a small reception area with a flimsy-looking brown table that stood alone and unattended. There were marks on the carpet to suggest there was once a larger, more elaborate reception set-up.

No one on duty; not much at all except the smell of old pig wafting through the air.

'What are we doing here, William?' Mark asked.

There it was, to the right of the table, on the wall, scrubbed out a bit now but legible all the same:

Streatham Hill Mental Health Unit

<u>*Please make yourself known to reception and take a seat*</u>

William flicked his head towards it. Mark saw it. His fist clenched.

'Should they be deemed *strategically important*,' William repeated.

As if on cue, they were interrupted.

'Who are you? This is a private facility.' A nasal voice came from down one of the pig-stink corridors. It belonged to a greasy-haired man in blue overalls; he walked double time over to them. 'I'm going to have to ask you both to leave.' Reaching them both, he stopped dead in his tracks. Something put him off. William knew what it was. It was Mark.

'Mr Fallow! I'm a huge fan!'

William stepped forward, chest out, and offered the man his hand.

'Mr Garrity, pleasure. You spoke on the phone with my associate. I'm William, producer for *Toss It with Mark Fallow*.'

'Of course. Yes, and yes again. I told the guy I was in. Are we doing it here? Now?' He patted himself down, his overalls making a squelching sound.

'Mr Fallow is big on grounding. He wanted to get a sense of location and authenticity. His first guest is a big deal, so the more he's familiar with your environment, the better. Isn't that right, Mark?'

Mark's eyes bulged. He muttered, '*Toss It.*'

'Great name; I've been saying it as much as I can. Live and breathe the brand. It's a good way to govern. Don't like it? Toss it.' Mr Garrity was beaming.

'Agree. We're big on the little man. No offence. The state makes men; we're sick of sheep, right? Mark is on a crusade to give them a voice,' William boomed.

Mark looked a million miles away.

The greasy-haired man was called Kevin. Of course William knew that. He also knew Kevin was obsessed with scandal and possessed a penchant for celebrity. Mark was his bait.

William made his excuses and ensured a swift exit, not before promising a further call to finalise date and venue for the recording.

Back at the car, Mark looked perplexed. 'I've seen him before. He was on the news.'

William smiled. 'He's your first task, Mark. That man might not look like much, but he holds the key to stopping Pierce.'

'Pull the other one. Him?'

'Kevin Garrity, Production Supervisor for Streatham Bacon Curing. Something's not right with the bacon, and you're going to help us find out what. I understand you've had offers to start a media career. A podcast?'

'Christ, never.'

'Never say never. I think a special one-off episode could do us the world of good.'

Mark protested but William held up his hand. 'Later. Not here.'

William and Mark got back in the car. For a few minutes they sat in silence as William let the debris settle. Eventually the question came.

'What did you do to get your envelope?'

William looked at Mark through the rear-view mirror.

'I killed someone.'

MEMBER FOR LUST

Breaking News: Workforce Growth? Free Bacon Rolls? No More Speed Limits?
Life under Pierce's Promise, Britain is Happy

16

Times were changing. The Labour Party had been consumed by the Pierce Promise, and the Cabinet Office in Whitehall was now the Centre for Rapid Policy Design. It had been perilously close to becoming the Centre for Rapidly Accelerated Policy before Renault had pointed out the issue.

Whatever people thought of Jackson, he believed in his mission. Every step forward, every little victory invigorated him. The knock-backs and the obstacles only pushed him harder towards the goal.

An easier Britain was in sight. A simpler country, one that would sail merrily into a golden future. Jackson embraced the fact the buck now stopped with him. Previous Prime Ministers weren't Leaders. They were little more than spokesmen for a shadowy, decrepit beast.

Stagnation and repetition were the accusation. Jackson had thought long and hard about apathy. Watched as the public voiced their frustration at politicians. He came to a different conclusion than them, though. It wasn't that the system was short of ideas. It was that the mechanisms to deliver were clogged. Jackson had unblocked the drain, and here he was delivering on promises. Whether or not they were what the public wanted or actually needed was not his concern.

After the monumental announcement of a referendum on the concept of Parliament itself, it was vital that Jackson continued the herculean effort of winning hearts and minds.

This was his singular thought that day as he stood wide-legged and hands in pockets, addressing Renault and his team.

'The public needs to see the vision. Where are we with the bacon rolls? They need a name, by the way; sodding Boris got his bikes. And the speed limits?'

Renault stood opposite Jackson. Screens and tablets were dotted everywhere: sofas positioned to be able to receive and process data and produce real-time analysis while trends flowed like waterfalls as the focus groups took over.

The target was new ideas to titillate public opinion. Every echo chamber of social media was repurposed to hothouse and spitball whatever Jackson and his team saw fit.

Renault barely took his eyes off his own device as he answered his Leader. 'Projections have us at capacity next week, but it depends entirely on footfall. Pierce Rolls, perhaps?'

'Good enough. Do they have to be employed to get one?'

'No, just purchase a valid railway ticket.'

'It's an angle on homelessness down the line, excuse the pun.'

'Agreed. Main commuter thoroughfares are priority, but we'll get everywhere eventually.'

'There was a line when I was young, ran through Whitby. I remember thinking the grime was coal dust on the seats. Probably just filth. Still, make sure if we say it's everywhere, then it is.'

'Something to note. From the data it seems that more are deciding to work from the office again, if near a train line. Of course, the speed limits being removed will have a huge impact. We've agreed the spend on headcount for the removal of signage. It should boost the employment stats next month.'

'Good. Free breakfast and a shorter commute. Who doesn't love that?'

One of the men next to Renault shuffled, made a slight

noise. It caught Jackson's attention, so he cocked his head and invited Renault to speak for the man who couldn't find his voice.

Renault shot the man a look of dissatisfaction before composing himself. 'Yes. There are some . . . some that have questioned how safe it is to remove the speed limits. At the same time, bacon is quite a divisive choice for those who choose not to eat meat.'

'Accident statistics—or the lack thereof—and uptake will prove our point. Make it happen. Same with the Pierce£; some are never happy no matter what you do.'

'You'll need a follow-up. A tricky second album, if you like, after these two.'

'An evolution to the Pierce£ sounds interesting. Crypto is far too ethereal for many. Let's make it real; what about food stamps?'

'Food stamps?'

'All the rage in the States. Not really a thing here.'

'Well, there is the Healthy Start scheme and of course Universa—'

'Bored. See, details and small print are for losers.' He gestured with one hand as if building momentum.

'Integrity, Renault. Food stamps have an image problem in the States. Soon cash will as well—the tired old dollar and the plump British pound. Corrupt, symbols of inequality. Now, we take the Pierce£ and tie it to sentiment: the stronger the support for the Pierce£, the richer you'll be. Can we get Tesco onboard? Perhaps a discount for those that pay with the currency. Union Jacks as barcodes?'

Renault turned to the other two. 'Get that on Reddit. Frame it as a single mum's idea.'

It seemed logical in the end. Thinktanks and consultants took time because that was how they got paid. White Papers needed writing. A good idea would come along and be sucked dry before it even made it to the Commons floor. Whereas Jackson knew that he had access to an unending maelstrom of opinion. His new policy unit was the people: throw enough seeds out there, fertilise with rhetoric and discussion, and something would germinate.

'Pace is a question mark. This is assuming that you want to deliver something every month.'

'It will be weekly by the end, but I appreciate we need time to refill, as it were.'

'Quite. It's two policy ideas a day at the moment,' Renault said. 'But Dean here thinks we can scale that up.'

Jackson laughed at that. 'Do you, Dean?'

The young man with freckles looked like a deer in head-lights. 'Yes, sir.'

Jackson rubbed his head at the formality and sighed. 'So close, too. Leader or Jackson.'

'Right, yes, Jackson. At the moment we curate each post in line with the persona we think will deliver the best responses. Single mum, weekend warrior, gammon, Karen and a whole host more.'

'To deliver . . . what did you call it? Turn-key one-size-fits-all, bake-in-a-bag policies. Original,' Renault added. Jackson detected a little too much sass as he spoke.

Dean carried on, slightly hesitant. 'Yes, that. It gives us something organic. But it's slower; all the debate has to go through process and analysis with us.'

'Christ, you could head up the Foreign Office with the way you talk. Get to it. What's the suggestion?'

'Go direct.'

Jackson didn't respond. Instead he walked over to a window. One obscured by the beam from a projector overhead. He pressed a button and the blind started to ratchet up, revealing the Whitehall skyline.

'I want the country to be easier.'

Renault looked impatient, Dean terrified. Neither said anything. The others with them had backed off, appearing as mere shadows against the far wall.

'We've spent centuries making it all rather complicated. And is it any better? Every vote is a choice. Every choice has consequences. If we can feed the nation good news every month—hell, every week—then we ride that wave of positivity and sentiment. Yes, some cars might crash, some vegetarians might get upset, but we can make it up to them the next time. You think this will work, going direct?'

'Ye—' Renault was interrupted by a wave of Jackson's hand as he pointed to Dean. 'Not you, him.'

'Yes. We've modelled a few ideas and it will be exponential. Before long, self-sustaining policy ideas, creation and ratification all within a contained sphere of influence.'

'House of Commons 2.0. Okay, look into it.'

'There's a risk with it,' Renault said after a moment. 'Dissident groups.'

'Examples?'

'Take Fallow. It worked for us in the end, but there was a moment where it looked like he might pivot to become some sort of influencer. If he had built up a movement with enough of an online presence, we might have lost control of the narrative.'

'But he didn't. And we haven't.'

'No, but if he did, if there was another . . .' Renault's words were terse. 'We need to be careful we don't over-extend.'

'Dear boy, is that doubt I hear? Fear? When you were getting dressed this morning, did you leave your spine in the wardrobe?' And then to Dean, 'Can we trial it for the referendum?'

Renault didn't flinch.

'Dean, don't look at him. Come on, can we do it? Full trial

run—get the public to tell us on X if they've had enough of MPs.'

Dean shifted on his feet, uncomfortable at being the piggy in the middle between the two heavyweights. 'We can do it.'

'Make it happen. Clear the room now, chaps, thanks. I need a word with Ren here.'

As the room quietened, the two men were left with the hum of screens and the distant sound of rain from out on the street.

'Cold feet, Renault?'

'It's not part of the plan.'

'The plan is whatever I say it is. This makes sense; this is natural. This is the next step. A system where you can make it all better with a tap on a phone. Bad day at work? Argument with the wife? Your football team lost? Vote on monetary policy or where we stick the asylum seekers. It's exactly what the plan should be.'

'He won't like that you've gone off-script.'

'Well, he can say that to me then, can't he? I think he forgets I'm the one in charge.'

'Are you?'

Jackson gestured for Renault to leave as he pulled out his phone.

The buck stopped with Jackson. Perhaps some needed reminding of that fact.

17

William had killed someone. Mark struggled with that. Given a choice, he'd relive his shame on *This Morning* every time over taking a life. If it meant he had to channel his inner Joe Rogan and host a podcast, then so be it.

'You're the boss, right?' Mark asked.

They were back at the Omni now, William having parked in a hidden garage. The pair had exited into one of the many hallways. William didn't answer initially. Instead he approached the painting on the wall. It was of an older man with white hair and mutton chops that would feed the five thousand. *Member For Wrath 1897–1929*.

'There's nothing set in stone that the Member for Wrath has to be the boss, but as it happens, most of the time that's how it shakes out. My predecessor wasn't. Herbert Walker was Lust, actually, but before that, invariably they would be Wrath. I say boss, but it's more like first among equals.'

'Very *Animal Farm*.' Mark had studied it for GCSE.

William brandished his ring finger, a large signet on it. Mark had noticed it earlier, as it bore the same symbol as on the envelopes he'd received.

'A nondescript symbol for a nondescript club, the stovepipe hat synonymous with that time. Most people don't give it a second glance, but to us it represents what we are: forgettable, nameless, members of something beyond the individual.'

He slid the nameplate off the plaque and where the word

'Wrath' had been was an indentation, almost like a socket. William pushed his ring finger knuckle towards it. He twisted as the ring locked into place and, with a groan, the wall behind the painting began to shift.

'Does every painting have a special slide-y wall?'

'Some do; I'm not entirely sure to be honest, I think we're the fifth generation of Members, give or take. What's that, forty odd? I've not checked them all. Come, we need to find Susie and Zachary.'

The pair wound their way around the warren of drinking dens and times past. The lunacy vying with the majesty of this place prompted questions from Mark.

'Who maintains all this? In fact, how do you afford any of this? Do you get paid?'

'Smarter men than me have made some very prudent investments since 1605. Horace manages all of that for us— absolute genius when it comes to accounts.'

Mark let his hand drag against the wall as he walked.

'Greed manages the money? My wife manages our money; not sure I'd last long calling her Greed . . .'

Mark missed her. They shared everything. Shit, could he share this with her?

William seemed to follow the thought.

'Mark, it's best not to involve loved ones with what we do. Tell her you've been called away at work.'

'I'm not even sure I know what we do yet. Derek knows people, Horace manages the money, you lead, Jessica drops envelopes through the door. Zachary? Susie? Me?'

'It's a little more complex than that, and I'm late for something. Go that way, take a right and then a left. Third door down.' William checked his phone and gave Mark a slap on the shoulder. He was gone, behind some hidden corner before Mark could even speak.

He tried his best to follow William's instructions, but he

couldn't shake the nostalgia of being lost in the local Wetherspoons.

'Mark! In here.' Susie popped her head around a corner.

The Omnibar truly was something else. Mark rounded a corner and was in another bar. Zachary was seated on a varnished bar stool with what looked like a fluted glass of champagne. Earlier it had been a pint. Different bars, different drinks, he surmised.

The 1920s Art Deco was spectacular: an ornate coat of arms, oil paintings and extravagant candelabras, all arranged against bold geometric wall panels in black and gold, with a large fireplace burning happily in the corner. 'Here,' Zachary said, passing Mark a flute.

Susie took up the stool to his right. 'You've met Kevin, then, I take it?'

'I wouldn't say met as much as been creeped out by, but yes.' He sipped the champagne. It was going down nicely.

'Gruesome little thing. Incel vibes.' Susie gave a shudder.

'It's my audience. My demographic.' Mark's shoulders sagged a little.

'Your particular fall from grace did capture the public's imagination,' Susie added.

'It's funny, I spent the past month at home determined not to sell out completely. But now here I am planning a podcast.'

'A fake podcast, to be fair, and to save the country. That's a little more palatable, no?' Zachary laughed.

Mark sipped again. The bubbles formed a question on the tip of his tongue.

'William said he killed someone. Is that true?'

Susie's eyes flickered; her body tensed. 'Not our place, I'm afraid.'

Mark took the hint. 'Okay. Where are the others, by the way?' Mark was used to having lots of people sitting around him at the Omnibar.

'Derek and Jessica are running the sister mission. Accident Statistics,' Zachary answered. 'This is a dual-prong attack. A pincer movement.'

Mark nodded, pretending to know.

Susie added, 'Horace is probably up in his study. I think William has him trying to figure out where Jackson is getting his funding from.'

Mark shuffled on his stool and took another sip of the champagne. He wasn't much of a champagne man, but at least this one didn't taste like a fizzy headache.

'Do you really think I can help stop Jackson? I mean, what good am I going to do if the six of you haven't found a way yet? I'd wager you're all a great deal more capable than me.'

Susie smiled. It wasn't sympathy, it was knowing. 'We do what we can and have to trust in what William says. Yours was out there for sure, but self-loathing isn't reserved solely for self-pleasure.'

Mark saw Zachary take a big gulp of his drink and silkily refill.

'What happened to you, Susie?' Mark asked.

'Weakness, theft, arrogance, but yes, I suppose Envy does sum it up neatly. I was part of a committee looking into ways to turn our cities *smart*. You know, that rush to capitalise on the internet of things. Using technology to improve environmental conservation, connect commerce, reduce the time it took to even travel around. All in our remit. I wanted more. I worked hard on that committee, but women like me don't get a look in for praise.' She ran her finger around the rim of her glass like she was circling the drain. 'Anthony Byers. He was hand-picked, earmarked, the golden boy. The chair of the committee. When the paper was published, they would be his recommen-dations, his ideas; it would be his legacy. The ticket he needed right to the very top. So I did something stupid: I leaked it to the press, putting my name on it instead. Here, take a look.' She slid her phone to Mark.

Mark was looking at an article in the paper. *Driverless Super Cities: The Future Is Here.* The article explained how cutting-edge new technology would allow cities like Birmingham, London and Manchester to fully automate all driving inside the congestion areas, bringing about a quasi-utopia for the local economy. The government was preparing a mini-budget to divert as much money as it took to get it off the ground.

'I remember this. It sounded excellent. Shame it never happened. Money, right?'

'I wish. The technology wasn't real, not then. Ahead of its time. We were scammed. Well, Anthony was scammed. One of these Silicon Valley types who lied through their teeth to get their foot in the door. Being able to say you secured UK Government financing meant they could keep the fire alive with the hedge funds. A modern-day Ponzi scheme then, of course commonplace in San Francisco now.'

Susie's name was on the article, and she was heralded as the pioneer who brought this to the table. So when it all came crashing down, she was buried with it. Anthony Byers went on to a Cabinet position. Taking the bullet for someone was one thing. Stealing it from its chamber to shoot yourself was another.

'If something is too good to be true, then it usually is. I didn't live by that saying before; I have every day since. It's an unshakeable pillar inside me. Never again will the wool be pulled over my eyes.'

'The bacon?' Mark understood.

Susie nodded.

Zachary eased himself back into the conversation. 'Susie tipped us off that something didn't make sense about the production numbers.'

'We looked into supply chains as part of the committee. So

when Jackson announced a free bacon roll on every single commuter train during the morning rush, I thought something didn't add up. 240,000 tonnes of bacon per year, 660 kg per day if Horace's maths was correct, which it always is.'

'Plus the bread for the rolls,' Mark added.

'Exactly. So it wasn't a surprise when Jackson passed his Turbo-Bacon legislation—'

Susie was interrupted by a smiling Zachary. 'It should have definitely been called that.'

She laughed and continued, 'So not a surprise at all. But what was a surprise was that the production facilities were operating at maximum output nearly immediately. It should have taken a couple of months at the absolute bare minimum. The only way they can be doing what they're doing is if it's not all pork belly that's going into the final product.'

'What do you mean? Like horse meat? Bit 2013 right?'

Susie took a sip. 'Could be. History has a habit of repeating itself. Can't rule out dog either, maybe even something more exotic.'

'And you think Kevin is the best way of finding out?'

'You are, actually,' Susie said with some certainty in her voice. 'He's a grunt, but he has paperwork, we're sure of it. He probably doesn't even know what he has or what he's seen, but the paperwork is the key. If we can get on record certification of what's being delivered and where, then we can tell the public what's going on.'

'This is his golden goose, the policy that buys him the others. If we can sink it, tarnish it, William thinks we can pull the whole façade down,' Zachary added.

'I'm with you, except I'm not following at all. How do I fit into all this?' Mark's grasp on the topic felt like the bubbles in his flute of champagne. Always floating away.

'Susie tipped us off, but I'm the man on the ground, the prat with the pint. I befriended him in a bar, a few phone calls after. He's partial to a sambuca. Do you know who he brought up multiple times as we got pissed? You. Mr Mark Fallow, the Jill Bradshaw guy.'

'He's obsessed with celebrity, with salaciousness. I think he would die if he got to meet you properly and better yet be on your team.' Susie said.

'He did seem to shit his pants a bit when he saw me earlier.'

'There you go, then. The good news is Susie and I as your producers, alongside William, of course, have laid the groundwork for you to interview him. In a fun, light format that the punters are going to love. *The Supper Club* meets *Come Dine With Me* fused with all the best bits of Katie Turner's bite on *Politics Live*. We'll get him in here, get the mood lighting just right and record.' Zachary clapped his hands together, excited for the first time since Mark had arrived at the Club.

'What?' Mark asked.

'You get him talking. He'll reveal what he knows.'

'Supper club? What am I eating?'

'I'll pour you another drink first. You're going to need it.'

'He's sent his own menu.'

'What does an incel eat?'

The two experienced Members just winced with sympathy for their fledgling colleague.

18

'Cooking is the application of heat to salt, fat, sugar and acids,' Kevin purred into the microphone. 'Is that okay? Are the levels good? One, two, one, two.'

Mark blinked as the halo light did its best to introduce migraines to his already batshit day. He looked off to the side and saw Zachary and Susie fiddling with the laptop.

'All good, Kevin. Keep going. We won't stop; we can always make it smooth in the edit,' Zachary said.

'Candid and unplugged. Lovely,' Kevin replied.

Susie gestured for the intimacy to continue. Mark was thirty seconds into his first foray at the Club and he had to think of something to say back. Zachary's words minutes before echoed in his head: *Speak like a person, and if you can't do that, try being a politician.*

'Application, you say, Kevin? Tell me then about your menu today and what it means to you.'

'Protein is king. Take our starter today, sardine terrine. Poach the fish before mixing the oily flesh with jelly and boiled eggs. Leave it to sit in the fridge. Bosh!'

Mark felt a sweat creep up his spine; perhaps it started in his stomach. He soldiered on.

'I cannot wait. A treat for our first broadcast.'

'Nice digs this too. What is it? Pub turned swanky conference centre?'

They were pretending to record this in another of the

Omnibar's delights. A modern-looking set-up that ought to include those electronic dartboards, Mark thought.

'Start as we mean to go on. But tell me, Kevin, *Toss It* is about getting to the heart of the issue through our stomachs. You've cooked your soul out and now you get to tell me what you'd toss from society. Each course is a pillar of your thinking.' He leaned away from the microphone and studied his guest.

Zachary had intimated that perhaps Kevin was a few spatulas short of a cookbook. That wasn't quite the analogy, but Mark's mind was at its cognitive limit as he watched Kevin and tried to listen to his answer.

Before Kevin spoke, his hand snaked out to grab one of the foil trays of food. It was dented and buckled. On arrival Kevin had assured everyone this was the optimal way to transport and consume food, of course; microplastics were a scourge we could all do without.

'Sardines keep for ages. Cheaper and healthier for you than ham hock. So many people today will opt for what's easy rather than correct. I work a full shift at the curing plant and then can prepare nutritious food for friends.'

Me. I'm Kevin's friend.

'So that's what the starter means to me and what I'd toss from society. Excuses. Let this be a living, breathing, healthy example of how you can manage a professional and personal life—and excel at both.'

There was no template for how to extract information about pork from a podcast guest. ChatGPT would time out at the request. Kevin had mentioned his work, so Mark thought it best to examine that a little further.

'Fascinating. You're at the forefront of Jackson Pierce's new initiative—'

Kevin waved a hand at Mark. 'You can talk about him? I mean, you want to?'

'Sure, why not?'

'After everything that happened, I didn't know if it was too sore, too soon.'

'Keep it rolling, guys,' shouted Susie.

Mark smiled. Kevin was right—this was very fucking sore and very fucking soon.

'You're at the forefront of Jackson Pierce's new initiative to deliver a bacon roll to every commuter on every train.' Stifling a grimace, Mark forced the question out. 'What was your *journey* like to reach this career zenith?'

'They made me go to the unit. That's how I got my job. You know where we met? The curing plant. I was made to go once a month to talk to someone about my *feelings*.' Kevin dialled up the sarcasm as he said the last word. 'And then one day, just like that: Jackson. Your boss—former boss, sorry, Mark. Well, he just swept it away. Legend.' Kevin punched the air. 'They were offering work, so I thought why not. Sardines are still the superior protein, mind.' He looked around after saying that. 'Shall we tuck in, by the way?'

A foil container was shoved over the table.

'We don't have cutlery, I think, do we, Susie? Do we, Zachary? Oh, what a shame, we can't try the terrine,' Mark said.

'I've got no issue going in with my hands. Works better that way. Can get a bigger block, more texture.'

Zachary shuffled around behind the bar and pulled out a drawer. Mark could hear a jangling—a jangling which made him sad. Promptly some knives, forks and spoons appeared at the table and Zachary managed a sympathetic slap on Mark's back.

Kevin went first and the smell was immediate. Pungent is a word said but often not understood, Mark concluded.

Gelatinous morsels flecked as Kevin spoke. 'Manners, sorry, but it's how real people eat. The yoghurt has set beautifully, minimal shell too. A success. What do you think, Mark? How would you describe it?'

Mark picked up a fork. *At least* This Morning *was pleasurable for a moment.*

Now . . . How would I describe it?

Mark would say: the eating of the terrine tasted like years of austerity, neglect and everything everyone else accused Britain of becoming. Political divides would be shattered if politicians were forced to eat only this. Wars would be ended over a single bite as the entire globe came together to decide how best to ensure this could never happen again. Minimal shell my arse, too.

Instead Mark said: 'That is quite something. What a delight. Thanks, Kevin.'

'Libenter,' Kevin said.

Mark thought Kevin was experiencing a seizure or stroke brought on by the terrine.

'"You're welcome" in Latin. I speak Latin, study it thrice a week.'

Mark looked at his producers. He saw them duck behind the laptop, doing their best not to laugh.

'A man of culture. Excuses, then; what made you pick that?'

'Epi—' Kevin picked some shell out his teeth. 'Epidemic, isn't it?'

Mark tried to look inquisitive.

Kevin continued. 'Everyone's lying to themselves about reality. Look at me. I've spent my life being told I'm not normal, I'm a freak, an outcast. I'm society's excuse. Blame Kevin and now blame Mark.'

Mark gulped at the mention of his name.

'But you did it; that's why you're a hero to many. In front of everyone—the mainstream media, the woke fools out there. Doing what you want. Excuses are for those who can't. So we toss it. Is that the right way? For a soundbite, I mean, or trailer.' Kevin was getting excited, gleeking little sardine missiles.

'Kevin, what I did was a mistake. It was wrong; I regret it.'

It slipped out. Mark heard Zachary cough.

Kevin's nostrils flared. 'No! That's just the machine trying to bend you to their will. Don't apologise. It's natural; it's Jill Bradshaw. She's a bitch anyway; do you see her on all these TV shows milking it? Can I say bitch?'

'Sure.' Mark wasn't really listening; he tried to regain his composure.

But it made perfect sense now. Kevin was someone that used the Mental Health Unit before it was dispatched to keep Britain's commuters happy. A profound sense of empathy washed over him. What was this? Where ridicule and disgust had been Mark's initial feelings towards Kevin, now he started to feel . . . sorry for him. How many more would be suffering silently? Or in Kevin's case, rather vocally.

'I've got a timeline.'

'Of what?'

'A second-by-second, play-by-play breakdown of each still from *the* video. Wankgate is brought to life in my flat. Everything from the initial concentration in your eyes through to the moment of protest.'

The terrine seemed quite nice now compared to the taste Kevin's interior design left in Mark's mouth.

'When do you want the second course, by the way?' Kevin looked around.

Mark felt uncomfortable, out of his depth and complicit in this man's detachment from reality. It wasn't part of the plan but he needed to go off script. That and the idea of a second culinary delight from this man was downright repugnant.

'What is it?'

'Thai green chicken curry.'

That doesn't sound too bad.

'Chicken breast develops more flavour as it matures, doesn't it?'

Dear god.

'Kevin, why isn't there any bacon in anything? Surely you get a good deal, perks and all.'

'Let's just say you don't want to know how the sausage gets made.'

'I'd really like to know, actually. You know a lot of stuff. Educate me, please?' Mark asked.

Kevin peacocked a little in his seat. 'I'm new to it myself but I picked it up quickly. We receive the batches of pork, mix them to tolerance and then inject the curing liquor. Because of demand we've got a few different suppliers for the meat. Some of it needs a little more treatment than others.'

'Why does it need more treatment? Isn't all pork the same?'

'I don't know; some of it's old and smells bad. We just wash that more before mixing it with the newer stuff. It's all injection cured anyway. Chemicals get injected in and then it comes out the other end all good.'

'What do you wash it with?'

Kevin pulled a face. 'What's going on, Mark? Why are you so interested?'

Mark went for it. 'Kevin, I think there is something seriously wrong with the bacon. I think Jackson Pierce is risking people's health. I think closing the Mental Health Unit to make more bacon, substandard bacon, is dangerous.'

'It's not substandard. That's not what we call it.' Anger flared in Kevin.

Zachary and Susie hesitated, unsure what to do. Mark held out a hand under the table. He could see this through.

'Wait, what do you mean? What do you call it?'

'Relivened.'

'You've brought it back to life?'

Kevin sighed and threw his cutlery down. 'We mix rotting

pork with fresh pork and stabilise it with the fluid. It's all perfectly legal, what with the new bill he passed. The lads call it legalised necromeat. It's no different to those microwaveable hamburgers. Look, I'll show you.'

Legalised Necromeat. Mark wanted to be sick.

Kevin dived beneath the table, muttering about the food going cold as he pulled fistfuls of paper and documentation out.

'Kevin, listen.'

'No, you listen, Mark. Look at these. You've interrogated me, snooped around about what I do. I have a job. You lost yours. Don't feel bitter that Jackson is making this country a better place. If the braindead masses want to eat this crap, then let them. It's natural selection, isn't it? All the paperwork is in order—verify it if you want. I'm out of here.'

That was an option? They could have just asked him for paperwork.

Mark felt stupid. Kevin got up to walk away, but before he did so, he turned and came up to Mark, who was still seated.

'You need help. This podcast won't last if you don't even care about the guests' content. Never meet your heroes, I guess. I knew I should have asked for a fee up front.'

Zachary followed as the angry Kevin stormed out. He'd need help navigating the maze that was the Omnibar.

Mark sat, drained, staring at the documents, terrine and cutlery scattered across the table. Susie appeared, sitting down where Kevin had just been.

She fondled through a few documents and, after scanning a couple, paused and beamed a smile as wide as she could.

'There's something wrong with the bacon, Mark, and you just helped us prove it.'

NO CONFIDENCE

The Promise Vote — Click here to register to take part in the Confidence of the Commons Referendum — Early polls suggest Britain has had enough of MPs

19

'Good afternoon and welcome to a special edition of *Politics Live*. I'm Katie Turner.

'Jackson Pierce—Leader of Britain like no other. His bold vision and idealism have reshaped British politics in just six weeks. His rapid-fire policies, each seemingly more popular, more ambitious than the last, and his ongoing battle in Parliament to redefine morality and service have captured the nation's attention. He's a friend of this show. It was here he first announced his plan to abolish the House of Lords, a potential knockout to the legacy of this country. But today we reveal the deadly consequences of two of his flagship policies.

'New legislation designed to meet the demand for bacon has allowed *pop-up* curing plants to wash and inject rotting pork with embalming fluid—the same chemicals found in the funeral industry. Worse still, these plants aren't new at all. They're using government-funded services, including mental health facilities and food banks, to support their operations.

'The question today is: do we accept this? Should the Leader of Britain be held accountable for the damage done to public life in the name of convenience?

'And speaking of convenience, we've uncovered credible evidence that the repeal of speed limits on British roads has led to a sharp increase in fatal accidents in just a month. You might ask, "Surely these are being reported?" Shockingly, the system that tracks these incidents has been non-functional since the law change. Coincidence? Conspiracy? Our investigation confirms Britain's roads are more dangerous than ever.

'Zombie pork and road kill: the true legacy of Jackson Pierce, or just gruesome speed bumps on his road to a new Britain? Stay with us after the break as we dive deeper into these claims.'

Jackson turned the television off. 'That bitch, that turncoat.'

He gave *Politics Live* his time, his precious time, only for Katie Turner to bludgeon him on the eve of the future. The referendum was in a few days; plans were laid. He slammed his desk so hard that a few flecks of dusty plaster fell from the ceiling in his Downing Street office. Jackson wasn't used to outbursts of rage. He took a few seconds to compose himself. He smoothed his hair and breathed deeply. He checked his watch. It was just after two o'clock now; the papers would be in a feeding frenzy for the evening editions. The ten o'clock news crews would be sharpening their knives.

He imagined Tara dropping the papers off on his desk.

JACKSON'S BRITAIN DIGESTING DECAY, A NATION WITH THE BRAKES CUT

It was the time lag between scandal and rebuttal that irked him. In a world where anything could be instant, the media would chew over this whilst his next raft of policies might fall on deaf ears.

His climb to the top was rapid, his learning curve steep, but he knew the ropes now. This time tomorrow there would be no choice but to push through an emergency executive power and push the referendum back. Control was paramount, action critical, but until the text came, he could do nothing—should do nothing.

Jackson slammed the desk again. He didn't need instruction any longer.

The legislation was a slam dunk. He didn't have time to cross every T and dot every I. Since when did people care about what was going in their food? And what, the public enjoyed congestion on the roads? That trollop Turner was right about one thing; this would be nothing more than a speed bump. Let the fire burn itself out, consume all the oxygen in the political sphere, and then he could march on toward the goal.

'Ungrateful swine.' This was a shit ton of bacon rolls every morning; what did they expect? He considered calling Tara in to repeat his excellent pun.

A vibration, the expected notification. And then another, and another.

> Referendum can be pushed back. Calm. Do
> exactly as follows:

He threw the phone on the table like he was rolling caustic dice. Jackson had been accommodating, compliant, even subservient to instruction so far. A considered conscious choice so he could get his feet further under the table. He was proving a success. When would he feel like an equal? He was the fucking Leader, the last Prime Minister soon. Respect was a two-way street.

There was a fast rap on the door. It repeated before Jackson could acknowledge it. He was sitting in his chair facing the window now. It was only Tara, probably; he beckoned her to come in.

His skin started to crawl as a voice filled the room. *Renault.*

'You've seen—'

'Accident statistics. How the fuck did that go wrong? I told you to fix it.'

Renault moved towards the table. His eyes narrowed. 'What do you think *"fix it"* means? We're pulling off a political pyramid scheme here. Buy-in from the electorate, show them *results*, and shove all the nasty stuff out of sight. That's fine; that's the plan. But it's created a ticking time bomb. Skimped safeguards, unmanaged oversight.'

Jackson stood now to meet the man he despised. 'Yes, you sweaty relic. Except we use the time to significantly and permanently alter the mechanisms of British politics. With the consent of the British people no less. The No Confidence motion. My *Promise Vote*. So by the time the noise is greatest, it will also be useless. What happened?'

'A shitload of old shit.' Renault looked away and tried to regain his composure. 'Our country has, or rather should I say had, a fantastic reporting system for accidents. STATS19 it's called, and it just so happens it's been unavailable for 93 per cent of the time since the speed limits disappeared.'

'Fixing it means turning it off. Excellent.' Jackson couldn't help but laugh.

'Absence of evidence is not evidence of absence. And it wasn't off, we just hid it in data lakes.'

'That's not a real thing.'

'I can assure you it absolutely is. The lakes were over-flowing.'

'Overflowing? Drain them, then.'

Renault gave a smile that his eyes didn't share. 'Blood, bodies in the water.'

'You're enjoying this.'

'No, Jackson. I'm here to educate you that your actions have consequences. In just a month there has been a huge increase in fatal road accidents since the speed limits went. Twenty-two per cent, in fact, which is an extra fifty-three dead, and that's not including serious injuries.'

'But it's not being reported,' Jackson said.

'It is now, after they—after it was found. But we've got bigger problems.'

'I know. I've read the text. I'll push it back.' Jackson wanted him to leave as soon as possible.

'No, you can't. The issue is the referendum. You made it digital. Poor Dean didn't want to admit his virginal eyes were bigger than his belly.'

'Do you assess if every staff member has had sex? Get to it.'

'He was crying as he explained, but I got the basics. The blockchain that Pierce£ runs on, that would have powered the referendum, was lazily devised. It's tied to positive sentiment. Collateral from your experiment to link the currency to food stamps. It was told to weed out dissent. So anything it perceives as negative towards the vote, it will ignore.'

'That's fine; that's what we wanted.'

'No, you're not listening, or you're pretending to understand. Take your own dick out of your ears. It will ignore ANYTHING. You wanted a moral algorithm that was based on integrity. It's learned that the referendum—*your* Promise Vote—is a force for good. As positivity plummets and we try to tell it to postpone, it won't let us enter the commands. No back door; a rushed mess of code that will take weeks to unpack.'

'Is that how crypto even works?'

'Nobody fucking knows, do they? I just listen to the nerds that speak confidently on it. It's like pin the tail on the pissing donkey at the special Olympics.'

'Meanwhile the vote will go live this week.'

'Yes. You're inviting the entire country, those with internet or even just a phone, to decide if we should push forward with abolishing MPs. Only the fulcrum of everything we've been working towards.'

'But it will pass; we'll win.'

'It would have without issue. And it still better do or it's both our heads. But now? Katie Turner's pretty little exclusive has injected some doubt. You need to fix it.'

Renault handed him lines, the spin doctor with his medicine.

'Wait—he doesn't know that we can't postpone it, does he?'

Renault stood, silent. Jackson moved around his desk and got in his face.

'Playing silly games, Renault? Compartmentalising might work for him and me, but little runts like you? Careful, old man; you might end up one of those stats floating around in your lake. Or just sink to the bottom.'

'It's not a real lake, you buffoon. I thought that you could let him know. Your cock-up. Your *adaptation* to the plan.'

And with that, Jackson was alone. Good. He poured himself a glass of a liquid most amber, most luxurious. The ice clinked as he sipped. Adaptation was the key. He picked up the phone and considered what he wanted to send. In the end he settled for acknowledgement. He'd fix it, he'd improve it and he'd get everything back on track. The dick-measuring contest with the man on the other end could come later.

He made a call and as it connected, he was back in the mindset. Leader.

'Katie, it's Jackson. You pulled your punches—pity. Book me in for tomorrow. I've got something to say about all this.'

20

Mark hadn't slept. The past twenty-four hours were a fever dream.

His tired elation was replaced by crushing guilt the second he stepped inside his house. It was dark, as if powered down. Lucy wasn't there. He pulled out his phone; straight to voicemail. He heard Chunk jump off the bed, appearing at the top of the stairs like a wise guardian. His glare suggested Mark had fucked up.

Standing alone in the cold empty house, Mark realised two truths. It was nothing without the love of his life. And he had neglected her. The warmth she carried delivered Mark through tough times. A second chance was what people asked for, wasn't it? Mark blew that when he became an MP. He was on his third now, and it came in the form of a secret society that saved the country. He always knew masturbation had benefits, but this was ridiculous.

William had cautioned against letting spouses into this new world, but Mark didn't see Lucy as a spouse, rather a part of him. Mark refused to feel shame any longer; he wouldn't be shamed by hiding this from Lucy. If he was going to be anyone, even a disgraced someone, he would do it with Lucy at his side as his equal.

It was one o'clock. The fruits of their labours were about to be realised. Mark switched the TV on. There was Katie Turner sitting calmly ready to turn the tide, ready to re-ignite the debate. She launched into her opening monologue and somewhere between pork and Pierce, Mark fell asleep.

It was Lucy's key in the lock which roused Mark. He jumped up, dribble on his cheek, as Chunk jolted away, swearing to have his revenge.

'Luce!' His voice cracked a touch. 'In here.'

He had so much to tell her, so much to share. But as she entered the living room, he felt the energy shift.

'Hi,' she said without looking at him.

He wiped away the slime on his face and embraced her. 'I missed you so much. How was your day?'

'Did you?' She felt tiny in his gangly arms.

'What's wrong?' He tried to take her hand and lead her to the sofa, but she didn't move. 'Are you okay, Luce? You're scaring me. What's up?'

Reading the room, Chunk jumped onto the arm of the sofa and offered his head as stress relief. Cats were good like that. Mark started absentmindedly ruffling as he tried to make a silly face at Lucy; tried something to snap her out of the hole she was so clearly disappearing into.

'I couldn't do anything. I tried, but—it was pointless in the end. Stood up in front of all of them, but no, nothing.' A tear rolled down her left cheek, and then another down her right, until soon there was nothing but tears. Sobbing and shaking, she slid down the wall.

Chunk reacted first; he pulled away as if to say, 'Her, not me, fuckhead.'

Mark was dumbfounded. He sat with her on the floor, trying to grasp her hands, but they felt rigid and distant.

'I tried to call you. I needed your help, I needed support,' she said through the tears. 'You weren't at work.'

No, he was out gallivanting, drinking champagne and pretending to present a podcast, while the person he loved most in this world was going through something. He didn't know what it was and that infuriated him as much as his absence.

She looked at him now and tried to gather herself. 'I don't know where to start. The Workforce Growth Bill, it's indentured servitude. Oh, and by the way, I've been sacked.'

Mark's expression changed, warmth superseded by dire concern. 'Sacked?'

The most ridiculous things sometimes turned out to be true. Like being inducted into a secret club for disgraced MPs, or your wife fighting corporate greed to protect the rights of friends and losing her career over it.

He fought the urge to hurry her, to bombard her with questions, but lost.

'What do you mean? Indentured servitude, like slavery?'

Lucy closed her eyes. Mark could see her picking a thread and trying to untangle it.

'Everyone's obsessed with the sodding bacon. But he passed something, his first week, the week you—yeah—well, it was that Workforce Growth Bill, remember?' She looked at him now.

Mark sort of did, sort of didn't remember. It rang a bell, but his face must have given him away.

'Of course you don't. Why would you listen to anything I have to say?'

Ouch.

She carried on. 'It had implications. Seb's wife, Anna, found a project document left on the printer in the board's office. A clear plan for living, a list of affected names with VISAs now under their control, and a column . . . one column that denoted whether they thought we were a flight risk or not. Jane had been planning it with them, cut me right out.'

Mark remembered meeting Seb at one of Lucy's Christmas parties. He was a warehouse manager that worked night shifts. Lucy liked to get in early; they bonded over omelettes in the staff canteen. He knew that, but he didn't know any of this.

Lucy explained that the board had exploited staggering omissions of oversight in Jackson's first bill. She dipped into her workbag, pulled a scruffy bit of paper out and threw it at him. 'There—read up. See what your Leader has done with his irresponsible bullshit.'

Mark felt sick. The key details jumped off the page in a grimy light with Lucy's context.

Companies can streamline VISA process for foreign workers.

This new process grants employers provisions on the control of VISAs.

Employers are guarantors of VISA status.

Incentives and tax breaks for companies that provide housing to foreign workers.

'Our workforce is about twenty per cent foreign nationals. They were going to use it as a means to boost the balance sheet. I was kept in the dark. I am—fuck, was—the financial controller. This is ostensibly a financial plan, no matter how disgusting it is.'

It was one thing when Jackson Pierce derailed Mark's life. But this reckless legislation was coming after people who couldn't defend themselves. And his wife was caught in the crossfire.

'I don't know what to say. I'm so sorry. How did it end with you getting sacked?'

'I spoke truth to power. Called them out. Technically it wasn't a sacking. Said I'd object and that it was a resigning matter. Jane just smiled and called my bluff. Fucks didn't even let me leave with dignity. Shoved my desk into a carrier bag and escorted me off. Ten years I worked there.'

'Fuck, if I had known . . .'

'Where were you?'

He dodged. 'You could have shared it with me before.'

She scoffed at that. 'I did; I tried. You weren't open for business. Lights were on but no one was home. After a while I just thought it was best if I got on with it. Fought alone. You had too much on your plate.'

Mark let out a noise, somewhere between a laugh and a cry. 'My plate? My plate was empty, for Christ's sake. The sofa or my boring job. That was my plate. You've been going off to war each morning?'

Chunk's ears were back now.

Lucy started to stand, her volume rising. 'Don't try to make me feel like the bad person. I was trying to protect you.'

'Protect me? I'm not a child. I'm not fragile. I could have helped. He fucked my life over too, you know.'

'My life's fucked now too, is it?'

'That's not what I meant.'

'Please, say what you mean. I'll listen. That's what a partner's meant to do.'

He pulled away from her. 'I could have helped; I could have been there. Any other day.'

'If you want to be there for me, then be there. Sorry, we've clearly talked about me far too much. Why was your day so special, sweetness?'

Mark had spent time pondering the best way to explain the Club. A cracking little anecdote, a serious plea for the future of Britain, even a casual plop into the conversation. *'Hey, babe, who has two thumbs and has been recruited by a not-so-secret, not-so-useful organisation?'*

'The Club,' Mark said, almost a whisper.

'Sorry, *the Club*?'

'I guess if we're trading truths, I've also got something to tell you.'

Staring into Lucy's face, all rhyme and reason floated away like steam from his fading engine. Mark could see the narrowing of her eyes, the pursing of her lips. He scanned her face: a total absence of understanding, an overwhelming sense of suspicion. He'd been swept up in the excitement of it all. Mark fumbled and panicked through the blunt honest truth.

'Okay,' he said, gulping hard, trying to come across more casual, more neutral. 'I've not been at work because I was invited to join something. A club.'

Lucy responded with bite. 'Like the Women's Institute? Skiving work to make jam, are you?' Her glare was sharper than ever.

'No, no, hang on.' Mark's voice cracked. He needed to calm the situation. The more he tried, the more his voice broke. Control slipped with every word. 'Let me explain. It's not a normal club!' There was nowhere to go except escalate his tone. She just needed to hear him, to listen to him.

'Oh? Is it a club where you paint little figurines? Mark's special little club.'

He held up a hand—that was new. 'Christ, just listen.' Lucy's look of disgust was tangible. He regretted it but strangely couldn't take the hand down.

'Sorry, *Macho Mark*. Go right ahead.' She folded her arms and forced herself back onto the sofa to make her point.

Mark jumped up; the tension in his body was too much. He felt like he was being cross-examined. He needed evidence. He spun into the hallway and rummaged for the cards he'd stuffed under some old gas bills.

He shoved the wad of invitations into her hands. 'I've been getting these through the door for a month. I thought they were bollocks until I received this one.' He showed her the last card that mentioned Jackson.

She wasn't interested in the cards; she was only focused on what he'd said. An inadvertent dagger had slipped from his mouth. 'A month? Are you for real?'

He pressed on. 'I went a few days ago. I didn't know what I was going to find.' He wanted to hold her hand, but despite sitting next to his wife, she felt a million miles away. 'Turns out there is a group of people. Disgraced MPs. They fix the country in times of crisis. Jackson is the crisis.' She blinked unerringly. 'They picked me to be their new Member. I investigated the bacon. I did a podcast.'

Another dagger.

Lucy's head flopped into her hands and she screamed a little. 'You're fucking kidding me. So you are selling your soul. Mark's shame is released every Tuesday, now with our sponsors, some shit meal delivery service.'

He felt his shoulders tense. His heartbeat was through the roof. The lunacy of it all.

Lucy's lips contorted in disbelief, her voice climbing. 'What the hell are you talking about? You sound demented, Mark.'

At that moment Mark didn't recognise Lucy. He didn't recognise himself or their marriage. Sure, they'd bickered before, even a few shouting matches, but this felt different, as if they were being tested. The exchange became like gunfire, back and forth until lethal contact.

'It's not like that. It was fake to get information. We're hitting Jackson. It would help Seb and Anna.'

'You didn't even know about Seb or Anna until two minutes ago. You're so full of shit. You're a hypocrite. I keep things from you out of worry, but you lie to me so you can play make-believe. And *I'm* the bad person?'

'I came home, Lucy. I came home to tell you about it. I feel awful, but I'm here now. Look at me. I'm here.'

A pause, then she looked up, her eyes glistening with a sadness that defied belief.

'You haven't been here for a long time, Mark.'

'What?' Mark's face frowned and furrowed.

'Oh, you've physically existed, sure. But here? With me? My husband? Absolutely not. You don't know how hard it's been, how many nights I've laid there just wishing you'd find yourself. Wishing you'd forgive yourself. That you'd come back to me. No one wants a carer, Mark. I get that. But what do I do when the person I love can't even care for himself? Love himself?' Lucy looked at Mark as if demanding an answer to an impossible question. When one was not forthcoming, she continued. 'I'm scared that no matter what I do, you'll continue to slip away, to have life pass you by. I don't know how many more crises I can deal with. The intrusive thoughts were hard enough, but now, since you've resigned, you've been a ghost.'

Mark didn't know when the tears came. His face flooded. The wheels of his thoughts turned slowly, but they were finally catching up. The painful truth was oppressive. This argument wasn't about the Club or Lucy's job. It wasn't tit-for-tat, blow for blow. He understood that now, too late. His wife felt alone, stripped of her partner in mind and spirit. Her vulnerability was laid bare before him. Mark's head sagged, his chin resting against his chest. His arms flopped to his thighs, palms facing upward as if waiting for some forgotten wisdom to fall into them.

There were no words for what felt like an eternity until three fought their way to the surface.

'I'm sorry, Lucy.'

The blockage loosened; more words followed. 'You're right. I love you. I'm sorry. I do want to come back, I just don't know how.' He didn't look up. The emotions overwhelmed him to the point of stillness.

He felt adrift. Alone.

21

e's Teflon. Nothing sticks,' Jessica growled from her uncomfortable stool in the Fawkes Tavern.

She was nursing a now-flat vodka tonic in the amber glow of the replica lighting. One of the lights was on the blink; no doubt there would be a silent replacement installed soon and without fuss.

'All that work we put in with the accident stats too.' Derek was helping himself to a refill of some dark ale. He eyed up the blocky wooden stool as if it were a soft drink and opted to stand.

'We've been trying to derail Pierce for months and for what? The culmination of our work has been little more than a stick in his bicycle's spokes.' Jessica built up a head of steam. 'Any normal PM would be out the front of Downing Street giving their *"with regret"* resignation speech. Yet he's feeding the nation literal rot; he's jeopardising their safety.'

Pierce had played the game to perfection since Katie Turner's exposé. A response in a number of well-constructed parts. Off the bat, stood firm and guaranteed the referendum would take place on time and on schedule. Jackson then marched into the House of Commons to set about tackling the zombie bacon grease fire. Jackson's speech was a tour de force:

'I've acted in the national interest to expedite, to streamline policy, to cut red tape, to speed up the economy. All for our happiness. A few bad actors have looked to immorally benefit from the oversight on food safety, which only strengthens my argument that

Britain is in need of serious life-saving surgery. Dare I say it, purgery.'

Jessica couldn't believe it. Literally, the pun didn't make sense to her. Jackson played the get-out-of-jail-free card, complete with an inane new soundbite too. It became a trending hashtag later, because of course it did. Notwithstanding it was already a word, he was making light of something that should be serious. This masterclass in spin, this vitriolic rebuttal of wrong-doing meant the masses aimed their crosshairs back on familiar subjects.

Over his first pint, Derek explained his theory: the public doubled down on its disdain for the 'system' at large and an easy-to-hate group in particular—MPs. These were comfier objects for anger than to pivot against their new heroic Leader, which included being angry at themselves for having been gullible in the first place. All Jackson needed to do was to point them in the right direction and tie it into his overarching rhetoric, 'Britain is in a crisis of morality'. Depressingly simple, in truth.

Pierce continued to put the work in and a statement was released an hour after his appearance in the Commons, unleashing a wrecking ball to the government department responsible for STATS19. Mass lay-offs, a full review of all technical failings and a promise of a new shiny website. It would publish the true statistics live and on the hour from then on.

Sure enough, when it went live, the stats looked as bad as reported. There was a kicker though, a secondary page also unveiled huge new economic productivity wins as a result of the speed limit changes. Manufacturing, logistics, retail all showing a correlated uptick. There was debate over how accurate this was, the validity of any conclusions drawn. But statistics were boring and debate passé. Shallow analysis led to deep certainty for many, and the deaths were deemed a reasonable and rational part of Jackson's growth plan for the economy. Unfortunate, of course, but sadly necessary. Jessica wondered if they'd say the same if the reaper knocked on their door.

Ultimately in a world where money speaks, and often speaks loudest, it didn't take long for sentiment to shift. And so the Pierce£ was booming once more, declared a victory for the greater good.

Jessica knew the country was angry; she knew that Jackson marshalled a popularity that bordered on obsession. And when it was just bacon or a gimmicky crypto coin, she did catch herself wondering if politics had just moved past stale institutions and the status quo. Perhaps the idea of the Club 'saving the day' was obsolete, usurped by a thirst for something new.

But no. The people wanted Jackson because the people were lied to, manipulated and pulled along in a game that would end in tears. They had sped straight past tears, in fact; it was already ending in death.

She was a million miles away as Derek spoke again. 'Esther Murphy doesn't sit right with me. That should have been our centrepiece. Instead we're off looking into statistics and trains. I do trust him, but William said we needed Mark to really attack Jackson and we did nothing with Murphy's death. His plan seems erratic.'

'It seems tepid, bordering on pathetic. I'll speak to him.' She knocked her drink back with a grimace. 'Pour me another first, please.'

Derek busied himself mixing the drink, opening a hidden fridge wedged between old bar slats. 'What will you say to him?'

Jessica became itchy as she considered it. Derek placed her drink down, and after a large gulp, her focus was absolute.

'I'll ask him outright what we can do to stop him, what his master plan is. I'm tired of this compartmentalisation.

We've done everything he asks, so we've earned a little more trust.'

William's office was down a corridor, two lefts, round a bend, and then a right down a couple of stairs. A seamless door hidden behind the portrait of Mr Fawkes himself. She admired the steel in Guy's eyes. Her portrait was somewhere around here, near one of the communication rooms. It wasn't a patch on this, though, which had an authenticity that bled out from the canvas. Imagine all that fire, all that drive, that sacrificed virtue to go to the end and then beyond with a higher purpose in mind. It might have been the vodka warming her, but to Jessica it was that thought that steadied her as she knocked briskly on the wood.

'Come in,' William's voice boomed back. 'Ah, Ms Campbell, how can I help?' As she emerged after a gentle push on the sliding panel.

She'd learned a few things about William over the years. Be succinct, to the point, remove the emotion. He had educated her on the meaning of brevity.

'We're not doing enough to stop Pierce.' The words came softly at first. 'Esther Murphy was murdered; let's use that. Let's rip this tumour out once and for all.' The words were harder now; there was a confidence flowing. 'I can get Katie Turner primed again.'

William took his spectacles off and placed them down on his desk. He was fiddling with various papers, but his focus was squarely on her. 'I'm frustrated too, believe me.' He opened a drawer in his desk and pulled out his notebook. He held it with both hands, worshipping it almost. 'But *this* is all part of the plan.'

Jessica felt on edge. She needed to get her point across; she needed another drink. 'The referendum is imminent, and if it passes then goodbye to Parliament; goodbye to everything that makes British politics, well, British.' She took a step closer to his desk.

William gestured for her to sit, reasserting his volume. 'He needs to deliver the motion next.'

'Oh, come off it, William, you know as well as I do the public will not stop until he finishes the job. We've been here before.'

He drummed his fingers across the face of the notebook. 'It's about observing, waiting for the right moment.'

Jessica continued to stand, her arms becoming more animated. 'Time is against us; surely I can't be the only one that sees that.' She could feel her face warming.

'I've studied every intervention, every save the Club has ever made. Years spent trawling through the backstory of one of Britain's middling and not-well-hidden secrets. And do you know what I found?'

'No, what?' She leant forward.

'We never fix anything. We postpone it. Hold the tide back until the first leak spouts again.' Jessica frowned. William wasn't finished. 'Continuity is our calling, but what if we've been papering over the cracks? An infestation of fleas that we've only dealt with superficially. The symptoms keep coming back.'

'It's not our job to cure it, just to mend.'

'And make do, eh? Patch it up. Delay it. And all the while be on call.'

'You know the role. That's not our decision to make. They have to be allowed to get on with it in the most boring way possible. But it's too much now. People are dying, they are being lied to under Pierce.'

'And yet the nation cheers. It's unified behind an idea. Have we ever seen that before? A leader that gets more popular the more they do?'

'You sound like you admire him.'

'I sound like I'm waiting to see how this plays out. He could be the answer.'

'What's the question?'

William didn't reply straight away. He paused, as if recalculating. Genuinely considering the question on its merits.

He placed the notebook down, opened it and spun it to face her.

Inky roots and vines whipped around the page. It was a network—no, it was an organism. A family tree, a lineage. She looked back at William. 'What is this?'

'Succession planning. Jackson might just be the answer to who comes next.'

'You can't be serious.'

He rolled his head around his shoulders, limbering up for what was about to come. Holding Jessica's gaze the entire time, he spoke in a calm manner. But there was a power to the words.

'The Right Members Club needs to change. We need to evolve. And I need your help, Jessica, in order to do it. You trust me, don't you?'

Jessica said nothing. He continued. 'Have I ever led you wrong, Jessica?' He hadn't. 'Jackson is like nothing we've ever tackled. The book has no frame of reference for someone on this level. Avoiding military conflict? Stopping an economic crash? Even preventing voter suppression? That's our bread and butter. I wanted to wait until we see what way the nation leans on the referendum. You're right, they'll go for it. Jackson is too wily an operator, too slick and has far too much momentum to let a little slip-up foil it. You're my right hand. My number two. I want to induct Jackson as the eighth Member. A Member for All. Every sin. An Omni-Member if you like.'

'After we've stopped him?'

'No. He doesn't need to be stopped.'

The words rocked her.

'Right now, he's the nation's hero. Every decision he makes, every morsel the British public eat up is a nail in his coffin. They'll turn on him; eventually, they'll attribute every failing in their own lives to the Pierce Promise. But he will be the Leader Eternal and he will be a permanent, unmovable, undeniable disgrace. No need to fall; no need to run or hide or be disposed. And meanwhile we will work not in the shadows anymore, but on the front line. We will direct the country.'

Her head felt light and her legs heavy.

'Think on it. Don't react. Observe and consider what I've said. The British people want change, and who better to shepherd them than the Club that has protected them for centuries?'

Jessica took a second. Assessed her options. She felt the overriding need to escape. To retreat and give nothing away.

'I trust you, William. I'm with you.' Trying to sound genuine. A gentle smile shared between them.

'I need you, Jessica, I need all of you. Thank you.' And with that the conversation was over. A mutual agreement had been reached. Or at least Jessica hoped it had been.

She found herself wandering the corridors of the Omni processing the conversation.

All she could think about was how William had lied to her.

TERMINOLOGICAL INEXACTITUDE

Breaking News: Click here to cast your Promise Vote—Do you have confidence in the Commons?

22

Jackson had no intention of being anyone's disgrace. It was this thought that drove him as he prepared for yet another appearance on *Politics Live*. The 'Jackson' set-up was a mainstay now of Katie's studio. How ironic that he had become part of the furniture as he looked to do away with all the trappings of British political life.

The director counted down.

Jackson sat opposite Katie Turner. *Politics Live* was on air. Only this time he was on his own.

'I do not hide.' Jackson couldn't get comfortable in the god-awful chair. 'I act decisively, Katie.' The lights were too bright. 'Yesterday you ran your exclusive on the bacon, on the accident statistics. This evening, I am here, standing tall, showing Britain they have a Leader who thrives in the face of adversity. And soon the country has their say on the future of Parliament.'

'Sitting, not standing, but point taken. And we certainly appreciate your time, Prime Minister. That said, I imagine it is quite difficult to hide when you are the government. No Cabinet, no minions to take the hit.' Katie purred. She was being glib, taking more liberties with him. *Prime Minister? The cheek of it.*

'Accountability, transparency and action. That is what people want. That action causes friction, and friction can burn.'

'Your response has certainly burned. Whole government departments culled. Legal action against the manufacturers of these chemicals. It was your legislation that created the loopholes.'

'It was an oversight. I have underestimated the depths our morality can plunge. That's why I'm here. Not to apologise; apologies are weak. Tonight I will announce how we ensure this never happens again. How integrity is maintained in perpetuity.'

'We're all ears. The country waits with bated breath.'

Jackson felt his phone throb in his jacket pocket. Defiance was a predictable response. At the start of his premiership he would have paused the interview; he would have consulted the screen as if it were gospel. Not anymore. His ideas were valid—more than that, they were correct. If he was going to be the Leader, then he was going to lead, not follow.

'The public is smart. They know the price of a pint of milk and a loaf of bread. Without doubt, if we consulted with them, they would have pointed out the flaws in the Food and Speed Limit bills.'

Jackson's solution to his problem was elegant. Like a space rocket he had needed the boosters, the extra fuel to escape the oppressive atmosphere. But he could shed it now, let it fall to Earth and be forgotten. Renault and his master; their master. Jackson was no one's puppet, and he needed to centralise his control, and he knew the perfect way to do it.

The excruciating discomfort of the past twenty-four hours had been a warning shot. He almost wanted to thank Renault; his staggering teardown of the Pierce£ algorithm and omission that he too kept secrets had presented an opportunity. It was horrific appreciating that man, but like a vaccine, it gave him just the right amount of pathogen to overcome the illness.

Taking a deep breath, without pre-rehearsed words, he went for it.

'The referendum is the start. In the future, why doesn't everyone have a say? Technology has bloomed right under our noses. Social media offers us the platform, the tools with which to conduct 24/7 fluid politics. How dictatorial that our voice is only heard once every five years. That the mechanisms of democracy are so slow and ponderous. We elect officials to represent us, but the truth is these people are no more qualified than anyone to decide the laws of this once-great country.

'Starting next week, every policy idea I consider will be voted on live. Discussion, debate, discourse, anyone can contribute at any time. With enough minds poring over every detail, the country will be in safe hands. As Leader, you guide my hand and we steer the ship together.'

Katie recoiled, her eyebrows raised.

'This is what comes next? You talk as if the referendum is a done deal.'

'A good Leader anticipates. I don't want to be left guessing. If it fails to pass, then we revisit.' *Good luck with that.*

'Replacing the Commons with likes and reposts. What about those without internet access or phones?'

'We'll set up hubs with connectivity. If people want their say, they will add it to the list of errands. Pop to the shop, collect your pension, vote on tax reform, all in a morning.'

'It will be mob rule.'

'Are you saying the British people can't decide for themselves?'

The director, just out of shot, started flapping and gesticulating. He wanted to go to break; this was off the rails even for the forefront of political entertainment. New unprecedented territory, unparalleled hot water for the broadcaster.

They're uncomfortable. Perfect.

'No—' Katie was interrupted.

'Do not cut to commercial. I want everyone to hear this. I put it to you, Katie, that mobs built this country. The savagery of kings, bullying of trade unions, revolutions and riots of the past. This is just the next iteration of democracy. The genius is it doesn't matter who leads, only who listens.'

The director was joined by Renault now, puffy and red. He was trying to barge into production. Jackson saw him out of the corner of his eye.

Katie kept focus. 'A convenient thing to say when you're the one left in charge. What about elections? What about who comes after you?'

'The people will decide.'

'Via TikTok.'

'If that's their preferred choice, sure. Perhaps in the future the Pierce Promise will have its own platform.'

Jackson could feel his phone heating in his pocket. He would check the pulsing device later. He would come round to Jackson's way of thinking. And if he didn't, so be it. Jackson was finished. He gestured to Katie to wrap it up. She took the hint.

'Jackson, Mr Pierce, I sincerely hope you know what you're doing. A country's future depends on you.'

'Soon it will depend on us all.'

Jackson stood up as the director called cut. No one spoke; the camera operators scratched their heads as their units powered down, drained almost. Renault was waiting for Jackson off stage. His face was ashen now, his words hissed with discretion and venom.

'What have you done, boy?'

Jackson laughed. There were still people around. Shame, as he desperately wanted to hurt this vermin in front of him. Instead he stepped forward, touching the tatty lapels of Renault's blazer. 'Ah, Renault!' he said loudly before leaning closer to his ear.

'I don't need you anymore.'

Renault looked left and right, stiffened as he tried to hold onto his composure. Then he leaned back to Jackson and breathed: 'All your ideas were ours, were his. Without us, you're a cheap whore.'

'Come, come, you can do better than that. You will tell Daddy, won't you?'

Renault's face changed—from concern to a grin. 'You can tell him yourself. He's back at Number 10.'

Jackson released his lapels and stepped back.

'Fantastic to see you, Renault. All the best for the future.'

One down, one to go.

~

The police, the staff in the halls acted differently when Jackson returned to Number 10. A sense of agency perhaps, or downright bemusement at what he had just done.

He dismissed the lumbering security staff by his door. It would be a scene if indeed his father was waiting there. Sure enough, as Jackston stepped into his shadowy office, the silhouette loomed, the mood lighting playing its role to perfection.

It was Jackson who spoke first, his desire to assert dominance coming to the fore.

'Slipping in here undetected is a feat in itself. I'll have to revise security protocols.'

'Perks of the job,' William said. 'You've made quite the scene.'

'That's it? You being here in person is such a thrill. I thought you'd rage and scream like that dog of yours.'

'Renault? He's just eager to please. As you once were. No, no use in getting angry. It's done now. I'm here to see how we can make it work for us.'

This caught Jackson off guard.

'I even have a name for your announcement: the #PiercePoll.'

'We'll need an online shop for the Pierce brand at this rate.'

'And what would the profit share look like?' William sat now, opposite Jackson's grand table, and gestured for him to follow suit. 'After all, whether or not you plan to continue with me, you can't deny I was instrumental in getting you here. You're the Prime Minister because of me.'

Jackson corrected him. 'Leader.'

'See, right there'—William pointed—'my word again. The Lords. Carmichael. Even the low-hanging fruit of the bacon. All me. And not withstanding Esther Murphy.'

Jackson blinked. He had been about to acknowledge his father's feats but the final name, Esther Murphy, had thrown him.

'You didn't think that was luck, did you? The perfect catalyst for your revolution. If the people knew that the Pierce Promise was built on a murder, a lie, what would they say?'

'You had her killed? Are you threatening me?'

'Oh, behave, son.' William laughed. 'We're far past threats. I'm here to advise you. Show you the play-by-play. You've put the power into the hands of the people. No, worse than that, you've put the keys to a supercar in the hands of arrogant tech whizzes who are building an app that lets the public drive remotely, probably drunk too. I don't need to threaten you because the truth finds a way. Leaks are everywhere, and that will affect the precious Pierce sentiment.'

'Parliament will be gone. So what if they turn.'

'People think you're on their side. But if you become just another politician, a morally bankrupt liar, then how long until the next Jackson Pierce comes along?'

'There's only one of me.'

'You were a result of convenience. Inherited power. Hereditary gifts. A father who lost his wife wanting to provide his son with everything. It just so happened I could, with great means and resources. I give you one warning: listen to me. Or I will replace you.'

Jackson watched his father leave, the man who had shaped his life since fifteen, the day he was scooped out of the children's care home. An orphan given the miracle of renewal.

The fact William had come, risked himself in the open, spoke volumes. He was rattled, worried that Jackson's diversion from the plan would succeed.

As he sat alone in No. 10, Jackson had but one thought:

I am no one's puppet.

23

The unsaid part of being adrift and alone is that people look for you.

Mark felt it, for an agonising moment on his floor when he was scooped up and rescued by Lucy. 'We will bring you back, together, I promise.'

It would be a journey. Literal in a way as the recoupled pair found themselves on the number two bus trundling its way towards Lambeth later that afternoon. The embrace on the carpet had been punctuated by a breaking news alert. The Promise Vote was full steam ahead. Registration had opened early for holders of Pierce£, cross-platform voting switched on. Nearly all socials had some way of ticking a box, giving a thumbs up or even just a smiley face to the idea of throwing MPs in the bin.

As Mark glanced at his phone, a text message came in. Jessica. A summons to the Omnibar most urgent. In parliamentary speak it was a three-line whip. She needed all members for an urgent debate. A new direction for the challenge that Jackson Pierce posed.

Mark wanted to show a new, honest intent. He simply turned his phone so Lucy could see. Inviting her in, where before he had withheld. As she read, Mark sat there, waiting for her opinion.

She looked at him and raised an eyebrow. 'You think they can help?' To which Mark simply nodded.

'Then go.' She patted his hand.

He stood and pulled Lucy to him with warmth. 'We go together.'

As they trooped up to the upper deck of the bus, they were surrounded by eager, engaged people. It was a culture shock, to be sure.

Where public transport would usually be a game of solitude, keeping to oneself, the effect the Pierce Promise was having on society was evident. Groups mingled. Teens turned around, talking to elders. Mums chatted across the aisle.

'Is this for real?'

'How are you voting?'

'Burn the lot of them away.'

'I don't have a phone.'

The novelty would wear off, for sure, but inviting people in made it all personal. The genius of being able to tap away on your phone gave people agency. A natural evolution from posting pics of your dinner to having a say on national policy.

Mark and Lucy stared at their own devices. In that moment, an abstention was agreed between them: they would not cast a vote until they had all the information, until they heard what Jessica and the Club had to say. But Mark had to admit, just a little, that the idea of this new future was intoxicating. The new way of doing politics intrigued him. Not that he believed it would work—hell, the evidence sat right beside him that speed and intensity could hurt and leave collateral damage in its wake.

Lucy showed Mark texts from Anna and Seb. It left a sour taste. Surreal in the tonal shift. A few days ago, Seb was joking about the state of breakfast in the canteen. Now he was worried about the state of his enforced living quarters at the builders merchants.

Lucy's question was simple. How many more oversights? How many more people would fall through the cracks? How many more teething issues would the country face until the people got it right?

Mark didn't have an answer, so she asked another question. 'Why do they call it the Omnibar?'

'Omnibus for *EastEnders*. Every episode. Omnibar, every type of drinking establishment.'

'Christ, I could use a drink.' She dared a smile.

Twenty minutes later, Lucy's wish was granted. She sat in a booth in the Fawkes Tavern with a G&T fetched from one of the more modern rooms. Mark settled for the dark ale as the other Members pulled up stools and sat around with drinks of their own. Jessica wanted them to be comfortable for this debate.

She spoke, her words causing visible discomfort on the faces of some. 'William wants us all on side. He wants the Club to evolve and Pierce is his plan to do it. He plans to make him an Omni-Member. The Eighth Member. And put the Right Members Club directly into power behind him.'

'Come the fuck again?' Zachary almost spat his drink out.

'She's joking. Right, Jessica?' Susie now.

Jessica shook her head. 'I went to him. I was unhappy about how ineffectual we've been on Pierce. He's been plan-ning succession.'

'That's not how this works.' Derek's words were low, terse. 'It makes a mockery of everything we stand for!'

Horace stroked his chin. 'Jackson would remain in charge? Officially, that is?' To which Jessica nodded.

'William says if the Prime Minister, Leader, Pierce—what-ever—continues then he'll be permanently disgracing himself week after week. So it would fit the'— she air-quoted the next part—'rules.'

Zachary laughed. 'That's good. Horseshit. But good.' He trailed off as he considered it.

Mark kept an eye on Lucy. It was a lot for him, so it must be overwhelming for her.

Jessica waved a hand. 'I know. The Club course corrects, mends. This is a fundamental change. But one I didn't want to keep from you. William wants us with him. That's the question. Are we?'

'No, we're bloody well not!' Derek snapped. 'He's lost his mind. What, is this why we've done nothing with Esther Murphy's murder? The woman was butchered to make a message. And we're here holding a parliamentary select committee. This is bloody pantomime.'

Lucy pulled a face at that. Mark hadn't had time to explain everything. He shot her a look that tried to say 'oh shit, yeah, that.' Although he may have just looked constipated. It was hard to know.

'Hold on a second, Strong,' Zachary said to Derek. 'William isn't stupid. He knows more than anyone about this Club and what it means. Hell, we've guided every PM since 1605. You yourself got involved with all that business with Major. If he wants Pierce as a puppet, maybe it makes sense.'

'It wouldn't even be puppetry.' Susie said with a slight eagerness. 'We wouldn't have to work in the shadows.'

'Exactly. We can't just dismiss an idea just because it scares us. We'd be Members without partisan loyalties, working for the country's best interests. Don't we want that? Look at where we are; this is downright ridiculous. Being a Member means to entertain the impossible, no?' Zachary finished speaking and gulped at his flagon.

Mark had heard this sort of ambition before. Polished to sound like public service.

Jessica thought on Zachary's point before she replied. 'His argument to me was that we've been doing nothing more than papering over the cracks. Keeping the patient on life support. What if we can cure them? What if Jackson is the mechanism?'

She paused, eyes fixed on the table. 'I promised my constituency a lot. In the end I got carried away with the bright lights. Power can be toxic as much as a tonic.'

Susie spoke again. Her and Zachary were feeding off each other's energy. Mark could see it make Derek wince.

'William believes in the Club. He believes in the mission. After all, it was only ever an interpretation from what we know about Guy Fawkes and the original Members.'

Another look from Lucy, another 'my bad' from Mark back.

'Society has changed—is changing as we speak. What if our reading of the mission needs to change?'

Derek threw his hands up at that. 'You're equating turning a blind eye to observing. Complying with the end of every-thing we've worked to protect as fulfilling the mission. Look at our phones.' He pointed to the seven devices face up on the booth's table. All were open on the voting page for the referen-dum. 'In a few hours, the country is going to answer the ques-tion. It's too late to stop it, and then what? We don't do anything to try and prevent the motion? Sitting here having a beer as Parliament ceases to be. We'll toast democracy as it burns on livestream!'

'What would your new jobs be?' A new voice, Lucy's voice. Mark tried to hide the look of surprise on his face. 'If I'm allowed to ask.'

Jessica waved the concern away. 'This affects more than just Members now. It's a great question. William would have us as something approximating a cabinet behind the figurehead, I think.'

'Us?' Mark said now. It was starting to click. 'Running things for Pierce? With Pierce? How would that work with social voting?'

'It wouldn't,' Lucy said. 'Something doesn't add up. For William to do what he wants, much would need to be under his control or influence, and that's not what the people want and it's not what people will have.'

'The people would vote, and maybe William thinks we'd be the right people to interpret it all. Elegant, no?' Susie offered.

Derek made a noise close to disgust at that. 'Us six figuring out tax codes and foreign aid. We're good, but weren't we all dismissed for messing that sort of stuff up?'

'We've learned,' Zachary said.

'We're unelected, mate.'

'No one to elect soon,' Zachary added.

The debate was descending into rapid back and forth between sips of drinks. More fingers, more volume. More energy with every syllable. But Mark's mind was focusing on something now. It had prickled him then, but too much was happening for it to rise to the surface. He sat back, chewing his lip as he tried to think.

Lucy wasn't finished. 'It feels a done deal, though. This referendum is going to pass and I can't see how the motion doesn't either. What does the Right Members Club become if it doesn't follow William into this new world?'

Derek glumly sighed and, after a sip, offered an answer to Lucy's question.

'A WhatsApp group with an enormous bar tab.'

Mark was back in Jackson's office. The memory fused with his car journey to the curing plant in Streatham. *States make men.* The words echoed.

As he thought, Horace cleared his throat and asked for quiet, for calm.

'I will not have us fracture at a time the country needs us most. I've sat in Greed's chair for forty years. Damn, I was here when William was inducted. A broken mess of a man. He earned his spurs; he earned leadership. He became a student of the Club and eventually its master. Methodical and telling with every movement. He rebuilt something in me I thought long gone. I'd lost faith in the order of things; the systems had chewed me up and spat me out. But William made me believe again.

'A black man embezzling, or so they said. To tell you the truth, I can't even remember if I did it or not now; 1952 was a long time ago. But it was enough to deliver me my invitation.

'William showed me systems could be redeemed with the right people behind them. So if William has given up on this system, then this concerns me. That he would lurch so recklessly and leave little but scraps behind is troubling. Without tradition and rules, then democracy is easier to bend and break. Easier to convince yourself in hindsight that the ends justify the means.' Horace paused his quiet, even personal, commentary and then fixed his ancient eyes on them. 'Mrs Fallow is right. Something doesn't add up. What William is talking about sounds like the end.'

Mark was ready now. He looked at Horace and asked, 'The end?'

Horace shrugged. 'Extinction.'

Mark let out a little laugh. 'I'm not making light of it. Extinction. Christ. Do you know, I was only an MP for a measly week. I've been a Member of the Club for less than forty-eight hours. Everything I touch seems to end poorly. No pun intended. I am the least qualified here, least relevant and most disgraced. Even my wife has more to say on this stuff. I'm a fraud. But I do have one unique quality. One that no one else shares. I am the only person here to have shared a room with both of them. William and Jackson.'

Jessica cocked her head at that. 'Why's that important?'

'It wasn't,' Mark said, 'until Lucy pointed out something doesn't add up. Derek too. Why didn't William want us to go hard on Esther Murphy? And me pretending to host a podcast? Come on. How was that going to stop Pierce? *The state makes men, the system makes sheep.*'

Horace stirred at that. 'I've heard that before.'

'Me too.' From Zachary now. Derek and Susie nodded too.

'William says that,' Jessica said.

'And Jackson too. The day he sacked me. He himself said he sometimes didn't understand it.'

A ripple of doubt passed around the table. No one reached for a drink.

'The same sentence, the same mission. Our new mission. It's not a coincidence,' Horace said.

'Bastard,' Jessica breathed.

Sobering looks were shared. Silence filled the air. There was nothing but the creak of floorboards and the gentle rapping of metal on wood.

Tap-tap-tap.

'A lull in the debate, I see.' William stood at the entrance to the Fawkes Tavern, fiddling with the signet ring on his finger. 'Perhaps I could offer my two pence before you decide what way you're voting.'

Jessica's jaw tightened. 'We'll hear you. Who is Jackson to you? Speak, William.'

'My son. I'll explain, but first you need to know about *me*.'

He stepped forward and began to speak.

24

At the tender age of twenty-six, William Purcell was an MP.

The Baby of the House. The youngest MP of the 1974 General Election intake.

Five years later, it was the Winter of Discontent, and William was putting on a brave face for his wife Linda at their local in Bridlington. The plan was a quick festive tipple, then back home. Besides, an hour without having to pretend he was a competent father was appealing. So far parenthood, the arrival of Tommy, had brought only a terrifying guilt. An overwhelming sense that everything he'd held dear and certain about life was wrong. The guilt came from how hard he worked to convince himself that his love for Tommy was on par with his love for Linda. The terror because he thought that made him a monster.

He held Linda's hand over the sticky table. There wasn't a need for words. Crackly speakers played inane Christmas songs as they both studied their drinks. The bubbles in William's lager slowed as the slice of lime in Linda's gin and tonic withered in real time.

There was tension in the air. Britain was in deep crisis. The deals that were cut to ensure Callaghan, the Prime Minister, got his majority were proving a noose. Trade unions felt betrayed as the narrow Labour government backtracked after failing to curb inflation. It was classic politics, really, promises made—and broken—about nationalisation of industry, about control, about wages.

He was ignorant to it at first, the way most people in their early twenties can wilfully ignore reality. Linda claimed he should go easy on himself. His career was just starting, for Christ's sake.

He only noticed the men that night because of the noise. The volume of their voices, booming loud. In the vein of a Christmas miracle, he afforded them the benefit of the doubt, thinking it might be a burst of late-arriving festive cheer. Coarse language dispelled wishful thinking. They were workers on strike. Out of a job as a result of the increasing industrial action. Bin men, hospital workers, train guards, their anger was raw, simmering. Britain was in freefall and Callaghan's government shouldered the blame.

The taller of the men slammed coins onto the bar, counting them out. Frustration was growing in William's constituency in the last few weeks. All of a sudden the walls of the pub felt a little closer together. He was still holding Linda's hand; he gave it a squeeze. He kept one eye on the two at the bar and spoke low for fear of drawing attention.

'I think it best if we drank up and headed home, love.'

She was always sharp as a tack. A quick rub of her nose and a glance over her shoulder.

'Oi, Lord Purcell!' William's stomach dropped. The taller man was turned, facing them from the bar now.

'Merry Christmas, gentlemen. We were just heading off!' William added a polite wave as he made to stand up.

'Got to choose between a pint or the bus tomorrow, you know?' The taller man thrust his drink towards them as he took a few steps closer to their booth.

'Yeah, that's on you, I reckon. Merry Christmas, my arse.' The smaller one had a smoky quality to his voice, gravel-like.

'I'm sorry to hear that, gentlemen.' William placed himself between the men and Linda.

'What would you know about sorry?' The taller man was close to him now, his breath a boozy fire hazard. The smaller man was older, his skin leathery. He remained a few steps back.

Pointing a finger at him, he snarled, 'We're on strike because of your broken promises. Your lot are carving it all up. We voted for you. Look where that's got us. Soon to be on the dole with a cold, empty house.'

William got a chance to speak. He didn't think it through. The words blurted out, his inexperience in the job on show for all to see.

'It's been hard, I don't disagree. My wife and I were just going home, but let me buy you a drink for your trouble.'

'Our trouble? It's your trouble, pal.' The smaller man joined his friend now.

The taller man jutted his jaw out. Split his stance. 'We don't want your fucking drink. We want you to pay us what you owe us. To do the right thing.'

'Let them leave, lads.' A calming voice from behind the bar. It was the landlord. William was ashamed he didn't know his name.

'That's it, fuck off, you coward.' Something wet hit the back of William's head as he was leaving. It was warm and slid down in between the back of his neck and the collar of his shirt. Bursting out into the freezing night air, they walked a hundred yards before he dared dig his hand into the mess of matted spittle and hair. It stank like cigarettes and cheap lager.

Outside, hands covered in filth, William felt overwhelmed. 'I don't know what I'm doing.'

Linda spoke with love. 'There's nothing to do. It's not your fault. It's a crap situation caused by Callaghan.'

'I'm their representative. And I'm sitting there drinking, doing nothing about it, as their life slides into the chuffing sea.'

William and Linda's house was about a five-minute walk west from the centre of town. It was barely another 100 yards before William's blood ran cold and full panic set in.

'Prick!' The unmistakable growl of the taller man.

They must have looped around the pub, flanked them at the side. There they both were, taller and smaller, at the opening to some tiny little lane.

'Come here, let's have a chat,' spat the smaller man.

William kept focused on what was important. 'Just keep walking, Linda.'

Footsteps, quicker, quickening constantly. It was a wide road; it gave the illusion of distance but it wouldn't last long. The taller man was closing the gap.

'Barman's not here now; what are you going to do?'

William didn't answer. Instead, he craned his neck to see what the smaller man was doing. He was by a low wall. His hands were on it. His small frame gave an almighty heave, almost falling over. When he steadied himself, William saw a brick in his hand.

Up ahead there was a skip. It was just before the junction. They could dive behind it, then make a sprint through Westgate Park that was just a little further ahead.

'Go—behind that!' he barked at Linda.

She made a dart across. They both made it behind the skip. For a second, just for a second, they waited. It was a second too long.

A noise, a hideous grunt. 'FUCKIN' 'AVE THAT!' yelled the smaller man.

William grabbed Linda's hand, yanked her toward the park. There was a clang of metal and a thud. He felt his hand pulled down like a dead weight.

William turned. He wanted to be sick. He probably

screamed but he couldn't be sure. Collapsing to his knees, his trousers ripped on the uneven tarmac. Linda was prone. She was making a faint noise, a sort of quiet wheeze. He didn't know what to do; he never knew what to do. His hands moved around her, undecided on where to go. Panic finally placed them on her head. It was slick with blood. To his right he noticed it—the brick. It must have hit the skip and rebounded.

The smaller man and the taller man were there now, gawping and panting after their exertion. All of the bravado, all of the anger replaced by a reminder that outside of this hate, they were real people. Any alcohol that flooded their blood was expunged at the sobering sight.

The taller man wanted to run. The smaller man was in a trance, though, jabbering apologies. It was a mistake, an accident. The brick was meant for William. It was meant to scare. William began to rise to his feet. This taller man scarpered.

The smaller man remained, with the temerity to take a step towards William. It was as if the man lit up, highlighted by some divine power. An animalistic rage overwhelmed William's senses and then his limbs. He cocked his right arm back, curled his fist and hit him as hard as he could. The harder he hit him, the better Linda's situation would be. A sickening mash of knuckle and jaw. Noise like the butcher carving up a roast. The man hit the floor second, his head hitting first and then again third. The bounce echoed around the empty street.

William didn't think about him again.

He turned back to Linda. He scooped her up, blood smearing all over his jumper. Her head was lolling from side to side as he bounded along the road, veering into the pathways that led up to the houses. Not many lights were on inside. He pounded on the door, screaming for help, screaming expletives, just screaming.

The country was on its knees; people were scared or maybe

just indifferent. A society absent in person and in spirit. He only needed one kind soul to answer, and in the end it might have been the sixth door that did. She loped back into the house and came back with a long-corded phone to her ear. The image of him cradling his bloodied wife had done the trick.

William was talking to Linda now. Bargaining with her to stay conscious. Thrusting all known hope into his guarantees that everything would be alright. The young woman brought them towels and water.

They wheeled her into Accident & Emergency, where the Christmas rush was in full effect. There were yelps, moans. He might have imagined it, but for a moment William saw the spotlight again. But this time it was cast over Linda. All of the injured, the sick, the doctors and the nurses were the audience. Linda the stage, his world helpless and fading.

They were overrun—his government's handiwork again. The few staff on hand were prodding and poking, discussing in hushed hurried tones. William yelled, blustered, to no avail, the idea of debate and argument useless here. There they sat: the gurney and the MP in the corridor.

Linda mouthed to William. She wanted some water. Dutiful and doting, off William went to find a glass of water in this madhouse. Before he did, William promised her she'd be alright.

It was a broken promise.

The court discussed the events that had ruined William's life like a shopping list. Fondling his heartbreak, witness to his suffering. They could go home to their normal lives.

The police turned up at the hospital. William didn't want to make a statement or press charges. He was broken; he just wanted to curl up on the floor and never get up. It was only at the fourth time of asking that the officer's question made sense to William. His face dropped; a coldness enveloped him. They weren't there for Linda.

The smaller man, that vermin. William learned his name—Steve Cooper. The punch that put him on the deck kept him there. Stone dead. William was difficult with the police. Shrugging, exasperated at their questions. This didn't play well with the jury. William was reminded to keep check of his emotions as he erupted, trying to plead, to reason with everyone that Steve Cooper was why his wife was dead. And yet they had the gall to size William up for manslaughter. It was just one punch. One punch for one brick; that was fair, wasn't it?

The days and weeks since that night moved at a glacial pace. His mind was always with Linda. People told him about the twelve stages of grief. His system was much easier to follow. Drink a bottle of liquor, preferably a single malt, and then another. Repeat this step until falling asleep and then go again. It was dignified; it was in keeping with being a British man. Talking about your feelings was a weakness. Bottling it up while drinking the bottle was strength.

The court heard how Tommy was taken away. Selfish relief. William wasn't fit to be a parent. He loved his son, but every time he looked at him, he just saw Linda.

By the time the verdict came, William was down and out. The subsequent sentence was lenient, all things considered. Two years, suspended. William experienced it all like he was floating outside of his body.

Professionally it wasn't much better. *The Baby of the House* was treated like any old common criminal by his party: ousted with little fanfare. Privately, his colleagues expressed sympathy, even some support for William, though it was short lived. There was no fraternity, no fellowship to fall back on.

All of this horrific media courage was not a good look in the run up to a general election that Labour looked uncertain to win—a Labour MP killed a working-class man—best to just come down as hard and fast as possible.

He wanted to drive down to London. To storm into 10 Downing Street and demand an audience with Callaghan—to lambast him. He was in denial about the country, about what it meant to be working class. He turned his back on the real people. Real people with no buffer, no insurance against the decisions their government took.

What good would it do? The hypocrisy of it all wasn't lost on William. He didn't give a toss about any of those things before Linda was taken. Somewhere between the second and third bottle that day he accepted that the government would be swept away, and in its place would be another one liable to the same mistakes. This Thatcher woman next. Over and over, again and again the wheel would turn. Futile, all of it.

Sooner or later, he would have messed up his career, he would have failed Tommy as a father, and both of those would have broken Linda's heart. The drink barely touched the sides of the pain he felt; only time offered anaesthesia. So it was that time that he waited for. Sitting there, day after day. People said that time was the great healer; well, William resolved to put that to the test. He'd mould into the fabric of the sofa, stare at the clock on the wall and openly challenge it.

'Come on then, I've got all day.'

William's eyes creaked open. The lids felt like they would snap away into tiny little bits. He tried to swallow, but the cotton-like grip around his throat resisted. Fiery acid swirled in his stomach to match the sound of the weather outside.

His hand reached for the bottle, which wasn't there. Strange. He forced his eyes open, tilted his stiff neck to see if it fell and rolled to the floor. No, it was over by the dormant fireplace. That didn't make any sense. There was something in its place on the table, however.

He swiped at it, grabbing at an envelope flat against the surface. Pulling it towards him, he felt a lumpy wax seal on the back. The seal was a dark purple, with an image of an old-fashioned hat on it.

William hoisted himself up to be half prone, grunting and wheezing as he did. He was about to throw it away when he noticed what it said.

Justice for Linda. Closure for Tommy.
Do Not Give Up.

He blinked some more, a lump rising in his throat. Could be vomit, could be emotion. Below the sentences, though, there was something else. A pub in Lambeth, London with a date and time.

He pulled himself upright now. The wind crashed into the trees outside, dancing limbs of twigs and branches merrily moving. The man that killed Linda was dead; what further justice could there be?

Yet.

His inner voice spoke to him. His car had petrol. London was a modest four hours away. In amongst the debris and rubble of what used to be his life, William went to look for his car keys.

Five hours when all was said and done, including two toilet breaks.

He sat there in the cafe, hungover as sin, stirring his steaming tea with the purpose of an overindulged Labrador. William fought off the fatigue and judders as best he could. He longed for the nip of whisky that had been denied all day. Withdrawal set in somewhere past Leicester and continued all the way to the pub in Lambeth.

A strange group of men and women greeted him. There was a young black man, two older women, and their leader, a man called Walker, Herbert Walker.

William was to be Wrath. He'd killed a man, whether by accident or not. His rage disgraced him, so the name fit. The Club offered resources, the ability to effect real change and influence events.

Walker was bashful about his stark message in the card. The *Justice* mentioned, he explained, was to ensure future governments were held to higher standards. To ensure what happened to Linda could never happen again. Closure for Tommy? A network of contacts of civil servants meant William could find him. Use the Club as a conduit to make contact. He fell for this old codger's gambit, took the bait hook, line and sinker.

All of this disappointment and mystery, however, added up to one gnawing idea. His head strained, shards of glass splintering every time it threatened to come together. He pushed through the pain, through the feeling he wanted to be sick all over the table

Why should William dedicate his life to saving a system that had shunned him? His mind picked up pace. He was exiled; the institution had stripped him of his one true love. It had transformed him into a shameful disgusting excuse for a father.

Here it came in earnest now. This Club wasn't saving anything; it was perpetuating a lie.

Walker told him about the Club's origins, about Guy Fawkes. He should have let the gunpowder all go up. Nothing changed, not for the better. The institution was fundamentally neglectful and spiteful. Walker spoke about effecting real change . . . William could deliver real change.

He grabbed the hand of a waitress passing by. 'Could I have a pen? And some paper.'

He felt something strange, fiery. This was different. This was interest, this was desire? No, something else. He began to sketch, crudely attacking the napkins with the crappy pencil until he stared at the semblance of an idea.

A long-form puzzle where William could take his time to acclimate to his surroundings. The Right Members Club had lasted for hundreds of years, the British political system even longer. The system needed upheaval; it needed to be swept away. That was justice for Linda. That could be closure for Tommy, maybe even a legacy. William didn't want a drink any longer.

That's what it was. His desire to drink replaced with a simpler one.

Revenge.

LEADER ETERNAL

Breaking News: YES 62% — The country has lost confidence in the Commons — The Promise Vote passes — Pierce to proceed with No Confidence motion

25

The referendum had passed. William was so close to glory. But he found himself having to change course, adapt and improvise at the eleventh hour. In a biting sense of irony, he needed his ever-obedient Club to heel.

In his planning there were contingencies laid out for the police, for MI5, even intervention from Russia or the United States—he'd never in a million years considered that the lot in front of him would grow a backbone. It just was not on his bingo card. It was a lesson to be learned. Miliband didn't expect a bacon sandwich to sink him, and there was that scruffy guy undone by his tie—multiple, in fact.

He placed his glass down, sat back and looked from each to the next after telling them about his past.

'Anyone for a top-up?' He tried to keep it light.

Jessica took her time before replying, even placing her left hand on William's. He eyed it before meeting her gaze. 'I'm very sorry for what happened to Linda, William.'

'It's not your fault, dear. It was a long time ago.' He looked straight ahead, tone neutral.

'That doesn't make it any less tragic.'

Horace looked at him. 'We could have helped. You shouldn't have dealt with all that alone.'

A dismissive wave of his hand. 'Too emotive. It was an event; it happened. The only thing you can do is learn from it and course-correct for the future.'

'But Jackson, he's your son? You said he was an opportunity. A chance for us to evolve. Not that you'd groomed him for the chair. How many more lies?'

William had known that eventually someone would put two and two together and make Jackson. That it was Jessica was no surprise. Someone was bound to wobble as they pussyfooted around Pierce, given enough time. Now that Jackson was becoming an issue, it made sense to bring the Members back into the fold. Compartmentalisation was only worthwhile if the hatches could open, the sluice gates raised. He was relaxed about that.

'Everything I've done, I've done in our name. Because I think it's right.'

His offer of evolution, of a seat at the table for the Members was true—partially at least. As long as it was the kids' table at a wedding. That's politics, though; everything's fluid, subject to change. Those were in the terms and conditions. Small print people. That was what his Members were.

'You've instigated a coup.' Zachary was glib from behind Jessica.

'You were keen on it ten minutes ago, Grim,' Derek shot at him.

'I got carried away. But I stopped. You should have stopped, William.'

William gestured to them. Inclusive. Sweeping. 'You've been led astray; no one likes feeling stupid. In time you'll see that it was necessary.'

That was the real joke, he supposed. People often fought for what they wanted, not what they needed. Therapy for the symptoms versus medicine for the cause. It was hard to distinguish what was a priority when in severe pain. It would become clear for them, just as it had for William.

Susie spoke for the first time. 'William, what you're doing is wrong. Surely there was another way to grieve, to seek justice.'

He felt like a headmaster reprimanding some idealistic

youths. They were wasting his time. But he couldn't resist the urge to indulge them.

'You can't see it because you're blinded by the status quo. But take a moment to think. Tell me—you all who were discarded—is there no part of you that is glad to see the back of it all? Intrigued at what your new stations may look like. Back in power. Some for the first time.'

Derek balled his fists, the stocky man. He growled at William. 'You're lying. You're—'

'Doing exactly what's been done for centuries. I'm just better at it.'

'Using your own flesh and blood? Was that always the plan?' Jessica asked.

'He was my son, yes. Now just an employee, a worry, maybe even a liability.'

William didn't know if putting Tommy front and centre was always the plan or if he had improvised *Jackson Pierce* and his promise somewhere along the way.

What he did know, however, was that Jackson was thinking for himself a little too much. Transforming him from the teenage orphan Tommy and shaping him into the Leader had been masterful. The vast network of technical contacts at the Club's disposal made light work of expunging him from most records. He didn't pretend to know how it worked, in the same way as he didn't want to understand TikTok. Ignorance had been bliss for a time. The plan had been to let the children stay in their digital bubble while he could have a proper crack at remodelling the real world.

Except Jackson had let the bubble burst and was now inadvertently ceding control of everything to *them*, the public.

Focus. Patience. Adaptation. His guiding principles in this role.

William didn't actually mind the idea that Britain could shortly vote on policies. Let the public govern like a bull in a china shop. It was the principle that Jackson had done it off his own bat and rushed the job. He could have ensured there were back doors, avenues from which he could shape the debate and control the end result.

'You lost control of him. An employee. Did you all catch that?' Jessica was disgusted, the look on her face full of disdain. 'That's what we also are? Just employees to manage?'

'Calm down. It was a turn of phrase. And besides, you know how much I value each and every one of you. Jackson has deviated. That's all.'

'So why did you come back? Why aren't you at Parliament or Downing Street trying to rein him in?'

'He needs the Club. He needs you all.' It was Lucy who spoke, hanging back, not seated with the others.

'Mrs Fallow. Delighted to meet you properly. I did hope it would have been under different circumstances. But yes, she's right. I need you. Jackson has hastened my inclusion of you. That's why I came back, open and honest and ready to work this all out.' The words took him back to the pub in Bridling-ton; he hadn't missed a beat.

'I don't buy it. Nice to meet you, though.'

William feigned retreat.

Mark put his hand up but quickly realised he wasn't at school so withdrew it and spoke. 'Esther Murphy. Was that you?'

Renault had assured him that no one would find anything linking him to Esther. The only evidence was locked up tight with William. The available facts were as such: someone burgled her, filmed her—and ultimately left her to die. Without CCTV or a time machine, it would be impossible to prove anything.

Of course, William knew she'd been extorted. Her suffering had been accelerated for the greater good, a means to an end. Renault was discreet, almost surgical. He might have been

Member for Sloth had things turned out differently, but he served better on the outside, a fixer with a cold-blooded temperament, part spin doctor, part Harold Shipman. One of the first men William ever bribed, and somehow still lingering, a perfect foil for his immaculate machinations. Another creation in a way, *Renault,* an old French name meaning ruler's advisor. These little games helped William keep focused.

'It was a tragedy. I won't deny it was extremely useful for Jackson's ascent. No more lies.'

'Says the man who's lived a lie for forty years,' Derek shot back.

Voices started firing at each other and at William. Anger spilled over. Jessica roared above the din. 'What's your plan now, William? We are not quiet. We are not subservient any longer. How does this end?'

William flashed a smile. 'The motion must be stopped. Jackson dispatched with. I need you to help me do it.' He leaned forward. 'There's a secret chamber, a Members' chamber, underneath Parliament. I'll call in a bomb threat, we'll get him underneath and remove him from the equation whilst I sort an . . . insurance policy . . . a caretaker . . . for the country.'

Of course, he had no intention of stopping the motion; he just needed to store his Members away until the work was done. Day care for children, under Parliament as the crèche. He had been so honest, so a last little bit of compartmentalisation couldn't hurt anyone.

'Listen to yourself. This is ludicrous. This isn't what we're about. No, I'm sorry, the Members are with me, William. We can't let you continue, not now that we know.' Jessica slammed her fist on the table.

A big sigh. They were so slow on the uptake. He laboured the point to them.

'This wasn't a choice. And you've still managed to get it wrong. I hate to piss on your chips, but that was accounted for. I'm actually surprised it's taken you this long. No wait, sorry, that's too much credit, actually.' A point to them all preceded his next remark. 'It wasn't you, I told you. I let you have it all.'

No one said anything. The tension was palpable. William could see the cogs turning and the scenarios playing out for each Member. Their playbooks were written by William, so he knew every possible angle. Dig up some dirt, look over the documentation, go to the media, find some leverage. They had nothing.

Jessica cut across them. 'We can go to the press. Explain everything you've done.'

'We've done, you mean.'

He raised his hands, miming as if writing with a feathered quill. Big and pompous gestures filled the air. 'How's this? *"Jackson Pierce the nepo baby. Installed into power by the shadowy club of disgraced fuckwits everyone has forgotten about."* I'm not much for copy, so someone can punch that up. But what do you think?'

Jessica grimaced. 'It doesn't matter. I can live with it if the truth is out there.'

William rubbed his temples, not out of any sort of wound or defeat, but out of pity. 'Oh, Jessica, I really thought better of you. But you're grasping at straws now.'

He got up, a slight recoil from them. The bar was only a few steps away and he really was gasping for a drink. He filled his glass, and as he did, he continued.

'Glass half full thinking, that is. You go all hot and heavy to Katie. Indeed she may listen, and there's some bits and bobs from the Club's archive you could furnish her with. Policy ideas, some rough dates. But what else? The sad story of a bitter old man, a disgraced MP. And there's the rub. The first question out of her mouth—out of anyone's mouth. *"What on earth is the Right Members Club?"* Nonsense of the highest order.

Desperate has-beens role-playing as people that matter. Excellent stuff.'

He could sense their frustration and anger growing. Now he wanted to break their spirit so that he could simply leave them in this hovel and continue with his plan. For that was the final puzzle of *the Right Members Club*. The failsafe in case all this unravelled, as it had been doing the past few minutes.

'You'll have to explain your actions. Your funny little names. Sins? Imagine the pearls that would be clutched. Sure, Jackson would face some blowback. But he's Leader. He'll have gotten rid of Parliament at that point if you don't help me stop him now. The media, the public, they'll have nowhere else to direct their anger. They'll latch onto these people who are telling them—with straight faces no less—that they aided and abetted a bitter old man, who has installed his orphan son as Prime Minister and broken all of politics. And when they dig, when they blow the cobwebs off your *Google* search results— which they will—what will they find? A woman who steals ideas. A man whose negligence killed an innocent woman. A pisshead junkie. A thieving minority. A sexual deviant. Oh, and of course their leader—the woman who hates the people.'

'It doesn't matter about us as long as we stop you,' Jessica said.

He nodded, taking all of this in before emphasising each word that came next, a cold ice-like disdain infecting every syllable.

'It's never been about you. You never mattered.'

He played with the foam encroaching over the top of his pint glass. They had nothing to say back to him, so he ate up the air around him. 'It will be a bumpy ride for me, that's for sure. But tell me, do the disgraced, disgusting MPs with no morals have a leg to stand on? Jackson has been pretty clear— sorry, I should say I have been pretty clear with the public that

Parliament has an issue with common decency. It will just confirm what everyone already thinks.'

Crestfallen. To a man, crestfallen. The conceit of their true purpose revealed. If they said anything at all, they'd just feed the national hysteria that William had crafted. If they didn't help William, then Jackson would erase Parliament. They had no choice but to fight with him. And when they did, he'd consign them to history, physically below the past forever. Fitting.

The Right Members Club would be buried as he dismantled the Establishment.

He could have stopped there, of course he could have. But the discomfort from being questioned, challenged and berated by these fools on their high horses transformed what he had intended to be a temporary truce, a reconciliation, into something cathartic and enjoyable. The second pint was going down nicely, and as he drank deeply he thought about a final twist of the knife. They were down, so why not a heavy kick for good measure, a payback for the inconvenience and boredom they'd brought him over the years?

He turned to Mark. 'I don't pretend to know how it works, but I'm told it's very easy to remotely switch a webcam on. The technical prowess of the IT bods has really improved over the years.' And then to Jessica, 'I remember when it was a bit of a job to get access to an email inbox . . . I did laugh, Jessica, I really did when I read them. Cabbage Patch Folk! Utter genius, and for what it's worth, I agreed with you. They are provincial cattle down there.'

Jessica's knees bowed just for a second. She caught herself on the table, her face ghostly. Mark wavered; his face sank. Lucy went to him, shocked as well.

'You're lying,' Susie shouted.

'No, Susie. It wasn't hard to engineer the introduction to

the driverless car company. They were on the grift, and you and your buddies were ever so eager. The cities of the future!'

Susie was crying. It had hit her hard, the weight of his words. Zachary embraced her. William scoffed at the melodrama. 'I had nothing to do with you. Zachy old boy, you were always a specialist in self-sabotage. Likewise, Horace old chap, bit before my time.'

There was a shockwave of disbelief pinging around the room, crashing back off the walls of the bar and cascading back into the Members as the house of cards fell around them.

'The Club needed Members. I couldn't leave it up to chance and end up with decent, able people, could I? No, I needed the worst type—the unambitious, the cowardly, the overly subservient type. So I picked . . . you.' He waved his right arm, showing off his collection of saps.

Another sip; he was savouring the moment. 'My make-believe Members.'

Derek smashed his glass into the floor. He marched towards the table and William.

'Hold your horses, Strong. You'll like this next bit: Francesca Blake. She would have lived. You would have been fine. It's why your envelope took so long to come. The optics needed to be right.'

Derek didn't reply; he just upended the table. A roar followed and William fell backwards, tumbling out of the chair and hitting the deck. He felt his cheeks redden and his heart rate increase. Cretins. Derek came towards him and hauled him to his feet with a surprising strength and poise for someone so diminutive. William's corduroys ripped; beer splashed all over his paisley shirt.

It all happened in a blur. His Member for Sloth leaned back, about to smack William with a big right, when instinct took over. The same that put Steve Cooper on the deck for good.

William's open palm sprang out as if hydraulic, the heel of his hand striking the base of Derek's nose.

No dramatic fisticuffs, no fuss. Simple biomechanics at work.

Derek's body went limp, hitting the floor with a thud like a sack of potatoes. Every noise imaginable washed over the room like a flood of vicious pain. Screams, crying, yelling, gasps that threatened to suck all the air out, they all rang around the room like a raucous circus. William didn't want this to happen, but there was no choice. This was on them.

He slipped away to the door before anyone could stop him. He left them with a final summons. 'Under Parliament. Be there. It's in your best interests.'

As he snaked his way back to the garage and his car, he found himself murmuring, 'The Right Members Club—pathetic.'

26

They say grief comes in five stages, but no one tells you that it can happen to five people at once.

In the Fawkes Tavern, denial, anger, bargaining, depression and acceptance were faces, names and sins fighting to be forgiven.

Each fall had its mirror, a virtue waiting to be reclaimed.

'He can't be dead. He's not.' Susie was shaking, her hands uncontrollable.

Again and again she paced around the outer edge of the Fawkes Tavern, replaying the scene in her head. She couldn't accept it. It was all a ruse, them all players in a stage act.

No one else was talking. She was lost in her stupor. William had made the introduction to the tech company—the company that falsified everything—the company she'd backed. He was bluffing, wasn't he? She fell into one of the chairs, exhausted, close to convulsing. Reality was a different world right now and she felt herself fall further away.

She looked at Derek's body, then at the others, who were bereft. Zachary noticed her and grimaced; a pained expression and angry eyes were hard to hide. A resolve coursed through her—only briefly, but it was there. William didn't do this to her. She did it herself. He didn't make her take credit for the report. And it wasn't her that was lying dead on the floor. Her overwhelming urge was to stand up and comfort her friends.

So she would put all of the pain away and get to work. Aware of her own face for the first time in a while, she conjured a smile back at Zachary.

Derek was dead and Zachary did nothing. Drink in his hand, he stood there letting everything happen around him. Every opportunity he'd ever grasped fumbled because of the glass in his hand. William had escaped; Zachary even watched him and still didn't act. The glass was on the table next to him. He hurled it as hard as he could into the fireplace. Smoke and embers filled the room. Glass shards began heating, reflecting light in chaotic patterns.

That wasn't enough; the rage wasn't sated. He lifted the chair and smashed it as hard as he could into the wall. It collapsed and splintered. Horace gave him a look, equal parts sympathetic and reprimanding. William had spun Zach a yarn for years. Every drink, every indulgence—a carefully crafted waste of time—and Zach had loved it, loved every moment of it. He found himself panting, his body flushed, likely from the exertion but also a sense of righteous shame. Angry for all the times he'd commended himself on a job well done. He'd thought he was putting things right, helping the cause. Doing his small bit. All a joke, all a lie now.

Horace was still watching him. He made a gesture at the bar. A drink to soothe him. Yes, that would be good; let booze take the wheel. He turned and went to move. But he didn't. He couldn't. The anger was there, but it was different now. He didn't want to smash or to hide; he wanted to put things right. William needed to be stopped, and whether he liked it or not, he was in a position to help. He couldn't be clouded by drink, the vice that had obscured the truth all these years. He looked back at Horace and shook his head.

•   •   •

It was Horace's fault. The least he could do was to keep vigil by Derek's side. The others licked their wounds around the room. Horace stayed. His mind bounced with logic and reason, trying to neatly organise the cause and effect that had led them to this nadir. Horace should have stayed upstairs. That was his conclusion. They'd won a pyrrhic victory over William in the truest sense. Derek lay dead and the Club was in ruins. All because he couldn't just keep his head down and stay in his lane.

Horace's fingertips lay gently on Derek's still chest. A foolish thought but, in case of a miracle, he wanted Derek to be with someone if he shook off the fatal blow and sat up with his big Geordie grin. Why hadn't he stepped forward and intervened? It could have been him; it should have been him instead.

Horace looked at the door, the exit to the bar. *That's it, scuttle off back to safety,* he thought. He could wave a hand, lean on his tenure and experience. Let Jessica begin to clean up the mess. Instead he found himself doing something quite peculiar. He was muttering a prayer under his breath, so quiet that a pin drop could still be heard. Religion had left him a long time ago, but here he was—praying. Yet it wasn't a prayer, it was a deal. Whether it be God or some nebulous higher power. *'Please, give me the strength to stay, to not hide, to help my friends. Take me at the end if you must, but allow me the courage to give my all to save the Club, and save these people so that they may save others.'* He looked at Jessica slumped, sitting against the far wall, head in hands, and corrected his ask: *'Help her instead of me.'*

Thud. Jessica kept banging her head against the wall. **Thud.** William had used her arrogance against her. **Thud.** Every idea, every petition to do more, to get deeper into Jackson. **Thud.** He gave her advice and focused her drive. She thought they were a partnership. *Thud.* She felt crushed now by the weight of failure. William almost seemed disappointed that she got so close but botched the dismount. That sarcastic smirk as he stood there lambasting her.

She stared at Derek. Her head throbbed miserably now. She felt her shoulders slump, her body sinking further into the hard sticky floor. Shame on her for making the same mistake twice in her life. It was a remarkable display of self-confidence that ejected her from front-line politics. She was always right; she could do it all by herself and people just needed to listen to her. Yet how wrong she was, and now a man she counted as her best friend was dead. She wanted to disappear.

Jessica saw Mark in the corner of the bar. Distant, standing alone. His face puzzled, as if thinking. They shared a similar grime from William's admissions. His webcam trauma, her emails. She'd made peace long ago when the emails were leaked, but now it was raw again. She lifted her head and looked at her team. They were broken. William was victorious, despite what they knew. She couldn't do anything with it, he was right. She was useless, and alone.

Except she wasn't alone. The Club was still here, barely, but they were still here, so they needed to try, or what did her friend die for? For the first time in a long time, Jessica resolved not to try to solve the problem herself. She stood. The eyes of the other Members turned to her. She needed them; they needed her. They would do this together.

Mark couldn't help it. Derek hit the floor and his mind ran. He didn't know him as well as the others, so he thought it proper to let them have dominion over grieving. His mind was on another path, a tangent that he couldn't stop. Usually the intrusive thoughts were to be banished, to be ridiculed. But this one was like a message. It was a plan.

He thought of William's revelation. The webcam that had blinked on in error was actually by design. All of this wasn't happenstance or bad fortune. It was the cold, premeditated actions of a murderer. He thought back to greasy-haired incel Kevin and his worship of him, which made Mark squirm with disgust.

Lucy was sitting on the bar floor beside Jessica, knees drawn in, her face blotched red from crying. When Mark glanced her way, she met his look and gave a small nod, tired but steady. It was enough. It reminded him why he had to think, why he had to act. Mark wasn't angry; he didn't feel ashamed anymore. Because it helped him see what was important; it helped him reconnect with Lucy.

He wouldn't hide, he wouldn't excuse every mistake he made by playing victim to his brain. It was too easy to blame everything wrong in his life on that. No longer. Now was the time to stand. He reached out, and Lucy was already on her feet beside him. They didn't speak, they didn't have to. He looked at Jessica. She was standing as if on cue. He walked over to a table and gestured for everyone to join him. He started speaking as his thoughts arranged themselves into a speech.

'I only knew Derek for a short time. He was a good person, a good man. I can't imagine how you must be feeling. But I can imagine that he wouldn't want us sitting around feeling sorry for ourselves.' Nods from the others.

Mark continued, his voice growing stronger. 'I don't want Derek to have died for nothing. More innocent people are in danger because of William and Jackson.' He closed his eyes and gave a deep breath out. 'I think I have an idea. But I need you all.'

The other Members all looked at Jessica. She looked at each

of them, over at Derek, and then finally back to Mark. When she spoke it was with power and conviction.

'Let's do it for Derek. Let's do it for all of the Right Members before us. What have you got for us, Mark?'

Lucy reached across the table, resting her hand briefly on his arm.

Mark nodded. 'We're going to write a letter.'

27

'Slow down, son. My knees don't work like that anymore!' Horace shouted from the bottom of the stairs.

United in avenging Derek, fuelled by doing what was right, energy coursed through the Club. Up and down, through different bars and different eras the Members moved. Alcohol-themed time travel, Mark thought.

Lucy was busy with Jessica and Susie, transport to Westminster and provisional wording of the letter their focus. Zachary was off on a call to a man about some embalming fluid, after having sorted Derek's body being moved to a local morgue. There would be time later to grieve.

Three random threads that Mark's obsessive brain was trying to weave. He wasn't sure it would work, but in the cold light of day, as Britain threatened to crumble around them, it was all they had.

Arriving at William's office, both panting, Mark and Horace scrambled around sliding the portrait name plaque and jimmying the lock with an old ring Horace found. It was blemished and worn but bore a remarkable resemblance to William's signet.

'Herbert Walker, bloody good man. Always thought this would come in handy,' Horace said, panting, as he clicked it into place.

The study was silent. It carried a heavy feeling, though. The air was thick with history, betrayal and perhaps salt and vinegar crisps. William had built a cult around the Right Members Club's history, one Mark thought he could use.

'What are we looking for, Mark?' Horace asked, fiddling with his spectacles.

'Journals, history books—a treasure map would be nice but failing that, something on this Members' Chamber under Parliament that he mentioned.'

'Somewhat fitting we have a secret hidden right below Parliament.'

'Where it all began, right? William wasn't going to just have us help him stop Jackson and send us on our way. I think we can use that—well, at least the bare bones of what he told us.'

Mark pulled a few journals up and started combing through them.

'We know he loves to compartmentalise. That's how he got away with all of this for so long.'

Horace got down stiffly and started rummaging through some boxes. 'Sadly, no one could see the whole picture. All drip fed.'

He nodded to the journal Mark was flicking through. 'You're writing a letter? More my speed than yours, no?'

Mark stopped a second. Horace was spot on, but that was the point. 'I figure William is very specific on his means of communication. It's digital day to day with Jackson. But he chooses to keep the Club's history physical, old.'

'A gambit?'

'Calling his bluff. He said bomb threat. Where do you think he got that from? Old Fawkes himself. We just need some props and an element of surprise. I'm writing one letter, making two copies. He wants us at Parliament. I happen to know there's a little post office there.'

'Yes, there is. But you'll have to explain all this to me again, I'm sure. Two copies?'

'One to Jackson, one to William. You heard how he spoke

about his *son*. For a man who worships control and planning, I reckon Jackson is a bit of a headache.'

Mark dumped the current book and scooped another from under the desk. He opened it at the last page and worked back this time.

He turned to Horace and thrust his index finger at the page repeatedly. Horace leaned in, his vision narrowing through his spectacles, making his pupils double in size.

Mark read aloud from the page. It was an excerpt from all the way back in 1725 by the leader of the Club at the time, John Aislabie, Member for Greed.

'The decoy passage serves its purpose. Only the Signet of the Leader may unlock the hidden aperture and enter undetected.'

'The passage?' Horace said. 'The one rediscovered a few years ago?'

'Yep, I was given a tour on my first day in Parliament. It's all been sealed up, but William mentioned it. That's where he wants us to meet. He told me in the car that the Members used to be beneath Parliament all the time. I didn't know what it meant then, but now, they said it was found with a bunch of political graffiti of the time. Members must have been using it for years to access Parliament.'

Pointing at the book, Mark continued. 'And look here, there's an entrance near Parliament Square. Of course it's down through an old pub. What would this place be without booze?'

Horace just shrugged; it was an impossible question to answer.

Mark caught himself before over celebrating his discovery. 'And we have the ring now.'

Horace took his glasses off and began polishing them with a silk cloth tucked away inside his jacket.

'You said about props?'

'That's where Zach comes in.'

With the drink removed, Zachary felt a new lease of life. For the first time in a long time he worked for the Club without it.

He got out of the rental van at the empty industrial estate and took in the smell. Greasy burnt pig wafted around, the chemically charged fragrance overpowering his nostrils. He headed for the door of the facility.

Not even getting the chance to open it before he was met by the matted hair and stained overalls of Kevin. 'I would have gone for the Vauxhall, sir. Not the Ford. Better fuel economy.'

Zachary nodded. 'It's got a tail lift, mate, that's all I know.'

Kevin took some persuasion initially, like a scorned lover. That magical evening with Mark still smarted.

The call earlier with Kevin was interesting. Zach and Mark spent some time at the Omni sketching out a loose storyline that would appeal to Kevin's . . . sensibilities. Half truths were always the best way to flesh out a lie. William had taught them that.

Representing a shadowy government agency, Kevin was being assessed for recruitment. The podcast was his interview. Naturally, he passed the initial test with flying colours, standing his ground when challenged on Jackson. He bought it. Of course he did. So here was Kevin corralling members of his crew as they wheeled the barrels towards the van.

'Do you need me to come down to Parliament to operate the fluid correctly?'

'We need you back here. This is a high-value site. We need you to keep it locked down.' Zachary winced with his back to Kevin. Not his finest work.

Mark's gambit needed physical evidence that would make William think twice. For Kevin, it meant that Jackson's government was under threat from domestic terrorists, and the fluid was the key. The chemical composition was perfect for neutralising the imaginary dirty bombs being smuggled into the country. Mark and Zachary cobbled some plausibility together from a few sketchy Google searches.

'All thirty-six barrels, then, all accounted for.' Kevin's men finished loading them up surprisingly quickly. Zachary almost wavered, but Mark was clear that if Kevin believed one conspiracy theory, he'd believe them all.

'Takes one to know one,' Mark had said. While in the depths of his depression, he'd believed that Finland didn't exist and that Paul McCartney had died in the seventies. Zachary just used to drink, but conspiracy theories sounded a fun way to escape reality.

Kevin slapped the truck once the tail lift was back up and snaked his way round to the cab's front seat. 'Tell Mark that I knew he was testing me. I never doubted him for a second. The ultimate cover: strumming one out in front of everyone. No one could question his allegiance after that.'

'Exactly; he's a national hero, and soon you will be too. Got to dash, mate. We'll be in touch, yeah?' Zachary turned the keys in the ignition and got ready to pull out of the car park.

'Wait, wait. Here, take this—it's for Mark. He enjoyed it so much.' Kevin thrust a damp package of kitchen roll into Zach's hand. 'It's the sardine terrine.'

Zach dropped it onto the passenger seat and watched it wobble far longer than anything should.

Kevin backed off a bit now, and Zachary could see him in his rear-view mirror, hands on hips, beaming with pride.

Politics always seemed like a distant, unapproachable world to most he spoke to. Something that happened to others, far away from the grudging grind of daily life. But now, in a bizarre twist, people were being stirred into action, not by noble causes but through danger, deception and the promise of sheer spectacle.

Is this what William realised all those years ago? That the

world of politics was given life not by policy debates or even civic responsibility, but by fear and manipulation?

Zachary studied Kevin in more detail. Here was a man invested in saving the country. All it took to shake him out of his apathy were barrels of chemical fluid, conspiracy theories, and—as he so eloquently put it—a man strumming one out.

Zachary turned out of the industrial estate as Kevin stood there swelling with pride, convinced he was part of something larger. As indeed he was.

A LETTER

Breaking News: What next for Pierce's Britain? no Lords, no Commons, no future?

28

Jackson surveyed the last, remaining MPs.

They were starting to trickle into Parliament, each heavy step a march towards an inevitable future. A nervous chatter ricocheted around the old Hall as the time of the No Confidence motion drew closer. It would be a merciful end for a lot of them. *Putting the past out to pasture.* Yes, that was good; he'd include that in his opening remarks. They would be the last serving MPs of their constituencies, a Parliament recessed in permanence and never recalled.

He gripped his phone in his pocket. William hadn't contacted him.

It left him wary. His father was a schemer by nature. Silence meant he just wasn't part of the conversations. Now he'd have to force a reunion, drag him out of whatever hiding hole he was in.

He had been respectful and appreciative of William's wise counsel, but Jackson was more than capable of carrying on his legacy. If it fell on deaf ears? Well, tough luck; Jackson was in charge now and no one could stop him.

The anticipation of impending conflict made him itch. It was stuffy in here, the gawps and sounds of the MPs too much to bear. He wanted to stretch his legs, so he went for a stroll.

He could see it all from here. The usual buzz of activity in Parliament was doubled today. Reporters everywhere, visitors staggering around, bowled over by the dusty history, and on each side of the Halls stood dutiful police.

Of course, none of them saw Jackson as he walked around his private lounge. The large flat screens displayed a crisp high-definition image of all that was going on inside. Even some showing the growing gaggle outside Parliament.

There were some who opposed all he was doing, mobilised and militant on the lawn of Parliament Square with their homemade signs and witty limericks. It would have been a mistake to outright ban protest—even though he could have. Instead, he fed the fire with oxygen, using his troll farms at GCHQ to corral an even larger group of supporters along.

Arm them with larger speakers, better signage and off they went. It was a chaotic swirl of pointless noise, but crucially outside and away from where it all really happened.

There was a knock at the door. Jackson wheeled away from the screens and cocked his head. William with the element of surprise? He brushed down his jacket and told him to enter.

Nothing happened. He called again. Silence unbroken, Jackson felt his irritation rising. 'Oh for Christ's sake, is this a joke?' He marched over to the door and yanked its old polished handle open.

Nobody. He craned his neck out and scanned the dark hallway. Some of his security detail were at the end of the corridor by the stairs but too far away to start a conversation with. Utterly bizarre, thought Jackson. He went to pull it shut and happened to glance down. A cream-coloured envelope lay resting on the musty carpet. He leaned closer, a garish purple wax seal staring up at him. Jackson bent down and picked it up, an unmistakable hat imprinted into it. William's little club.

So he was here, nearby, playing with him.

Retreating back into his private lounge, he opened the envelope in one swift motion and slid the contents out. It was a folded letter along with a small tough piece of card. The card had some over-the-top purple embroidery. His father wasted his time with haberdashery, it seemed. If the old man wanted to fanny about with arts and crafts, then Jackson was more than happy to oblige with retirement.

The card contained a message. He began to read it.

Jackson – we found this with your father's things
Didn't want you to look weak
Love, Mark Fallow 'The Wanker'
Member for Lust

William had bungled it. Instead he was now holding something incendiary, he could feel it.

He unfolded the letter. If he thought that Fallow reaching out was a shock, then what followed almost put him on the floor. Heart rate increasing, he scanned, his eyes darting from one sentence to another as a cruel picture emerged.

. . . Renault, he can track the messages. The Club has discovered the truth. They know Jackson is my son, they will leak it to the press . . .

. . . Jackson has gone off script. He has become a liability . . .

. . . he needs to be disposed of in a way that makes him a martyr, it will be better for the plan . . .

. . . we can put anyone in we want after some time has passed, but once Parliament is dissolved, do it then . . .

. . . get him under the Commons, lure him after the bomb threat . . .

The letter fell from his hands. His fists clenched as his jaw tightened. A cold wave washed over him. William . . . was going to butcher him like cattle.

Renault was never just a crooked spin doctor; he was his father's ripcord. For a second, just a second, he wasn't Jackson, he was Tommy again. He remembered the cold nights, the isolation and the fear that life was passing him by. It was overwhelming. He felt faint.

That was a long time ago. Things were different now that he was Jackson Pierce. He had the starry touch. He was the Leader of this country, and no old man and his vulture would stop him.

He reached for the letter on the floor and folded it slowly, the weight of what came next sinking in. He was alone, finally alone. If the old man wanted to make up for years of neglect by playing games with his son, then Jackson would oblige him. The panic he'd felt before melted away and was replaced with a cold focus. His father's words wouldn't be his end. He pulled his phone out and sent a text to William.

> You've failed. Your Club is here.

They would just be another obstacle to remove.

29

William had the passages committed to memory.

It meant that slipping into the Speaker's office was no trouble at all. Rachel Jenkins stood there, looking in the mirror, eyes closed, reciting her opening remarks, her voice wavering alongside her greying brown hair which had seen better days.

William caught a glimpse of himself in the same reflection; his exhaustion was inescapable. Still, there was work to be done and errands to carry out. It was full circle in a way, here on the day that it all stopped.

Rachel went over her speech again, the tone sombre now. 'I call on this Chamber to vote on the motion that this government has no confidence in this House.'

William coughed. Rachel's eyes snapped open and their eyes met in the mirror. 'Alien, isn't it? We've become so used to the usual wording.'

'Sorry, who are you?'

'A friend, an advisor of sorts, if you like.'

Rachel turned sharply. 'Jackson takes advice? That's news to me. You don't work for him.'

William smiled with a nod. She was bright. 'No, Madam Speaker. I work for no one, serve no leader, no party. Today I am here for . . . well, you.'

'For me?' Rachel scoffed. 'I'm the Speaker of Parliament, the last Parliament about to be voted out of existence. You're here for a photo?'

He wandered around the room, grazing various papers and books with his fingertips. He spoke calmly. 'Opportunity, actually. There are people who watch, and there are people who do. I think you're one who does.'

Rachel stiffened, her posture defensive. 'Does nothing, more like. He's relegated me to cheerleader.'

William clicked his fingers as if a lightbulb had illuminated. 'And nothing is exactly what I want you to do today.'

'You didn't have to come all this way, then. Now please leave before I call security.'

William tilted his head. The game of cat and mouse was numbing. 'You play your role well. You really do. But you're let down by this place. It is a cesspit of rats, leaky like the roof. I've heard a rumour. More whispers, I suppose. Rachel Jenkins rallying last-minute opposition to stop the vote. A backbone in the final moments.'

He got closer to her and dropped any sense of kindness from his tone.

'Come now, at best, a Speaker can make a nuisance of themselves. Only delay the inevitable.'

She didn't back down or flinch. She bit back.

'If it's inevitable, why are you here?'

'You're flinging stones at a battleship. Arrows at a tank. All that politicking, it will be for nothing.' He lowered himself into one of the old uncomfortable chairs without a flicker of dismay. 'Momentum is king. Stop him today and Jackson will come back. Again and again. He's relentless, and with the power he holds, stopping him now won't just be difficult, it'll be impossible. But you . . .' He traced a finger over her outline, '. . . you won't come back.'

She was unmoved, her voice strong. 'Is that a threat?'

'No, no, goodness, no. It's a warning,' William said.

Rachel ran her hands through her hair as if doing some horrible maths.

'So I act and I'm finished. Or I do nothing and democracy is. I let this farce play out and what changes? It's like asking me to pick which child should die.'

'The weaker one, obviously.'

She recoiled at the remark and waved a dismissive hand in frustration. 'The end result is the same either way. Jackson wins, Parliament falls, and I become a footnote in the obituary.'

'Not if you take my deal,' William replied sweetly. 'Jackson has been useful to a point, but a Prime Minister can only take so much trauma regardless of how he navigates it. Brexit, Covid, cost of living crisis, even war. Eventually something has to give. It does for everyone else and it will for him. After this exertion he'll be at his weakest. Having achieved his aims, there is nowhere to hide, no one else to blame. Take a step back, Rachel, and see the bigger picture. You can't beat him today, but you can absolutely lose.'

'What do you want from me? And what do I get in return? Just so we're clear.'

'Let the vote proceed unimpeded. Call off your bloc. In return, I'll furnish you with the weaponry to stop him once and for all. Evidence, for clarity's sake. The kind that doesn't just bounce off but destroys.'

She shook her head undecidedly. 'No one can take him down.'

'I can.' His confidence was absolute.

Rachel was caught in two minds. She was desperate. 'Why me?'

'Good question. You're really very astute.' William licked his lips before continuing. Biting down, he jabbed a finger at her. 'You're a failure. You've been benched, humiliated, derided and insulted by him at every turn. And yet you stayed. That makes you useful to a man like me. I've made a life of working with people like that, the ones that others overlook. Your sin is inaction, dithering. A sloth in that lofty chair above proceedings.'

Her face reddened, deeply embarrassed. No words came back at him.

He stood up, his work just about done here. 'Play along, play a role for me and you'll be more than a footnote of a broken system. You'll be the steward of a new Britain. Once he's gone, someone has to steer the ship. There needs to be a new system. A new democracy if you like, just with less. Shaped as we see fit. Your legacy, my vision.'

Rachel was stunned. She uttered a final question. 'And if I stop the motion?'

'Then Jackson wins. And you . . . well, it was nice to have met you.'

He opened the door and walked through it without another look. 'Make the right choice, Madam Speaker.'

While William walked away from the office, taking a few sharp turns around the corridors, weaving in and around people, Renault was tasked with stalking below. The intention was to cut off whatever the Club were planning, if they were planning anything at all. The useless reprobates were probably still wallowing over Derek Strong.

As long as the motion passed, the Club could do whatever they wanted. After that, he could pick them off one by one. The idea of Katie Turner taking them to task appealed. Jessica's own mouth putting the Members' proverbial feet in it again.

'Excuse me, are you William Purcell?' A voice from behind him. William almost tripped with the shock of hearing his full name uttered in this place. He had walked the halls of Parliament anonymously for many a year.

He turned and saw a young man behind the Post Office counter, waving an envelope at him. 'Yes, who's asking?'

He was busy doing a number of other things already, his

eyes barely lingering on William for more than a second. Completely disinterested.

'Oh, it is you. There was a picture dropped off with this envelope.'

'Who dropped it off?' William demanded.

The young man, with his back to William, nonchalantly replied, 'Some guy a minute ago, said you'd be around here.'

His patience was non existent. 'Who, for fuck's sake?'

'Whoa, calm down, granddad, I don't know—just a guy, didn't give his name.' The boy was defensive now and clearly wasn't helpful or willing to continue the exchange and went back to the various piles of letters to administer.

William knew at once what game was afoot here. The unmistakable envelope of the Right Members Club. Every sinew told him to get to a passage and open it in seclusion. Instead he found himself ripping it open and scratching at the contents.

It was a letter. A handwritten letter, but it wasn't to him at all but rather from him to Renault. He laughed, scanning it a couple of times before crumpling it up.

The charlatans! How dare they try to play with him and with such a cheap imitation. Flattery, in a way. An obvious ploy to drive a wedge between him and Jackson at the critical moment.

As if on cue his phone buzzed three times in his pocket. He knew that meant a text from Jackson.

You've failed. Your Club is here.

He ran his knuckle along his nose, taking it all in and calibrating the next move. So the Members' plan amounted to duplicate letters. A confrontation and awkwardness between William and Jackson. A retread of what sparked the Club into existence.

No matter; this would be easy to clear up. Jackson would fly off the handle, no doubt. A temper tantrum for the ages, but

William could soothe him, would calm him down. Logic and reason would prevail once he showed him the duplicate letter he'd received. Nothing more than foolish bait, a fun—if short-sighted—trick.

Close to replying, a second message came through—only one buzz this time—Renault.

It was a picture message, a grainy sort of CCTV image. A sorry-looking van full of objects, with a man lifting something onto a sack barrow. William pinched the screen to zoom in. His irritation bristled as he made out the unmistakable curls of Grim in amongst what were now clearly barrels.

He zoomed in further to the top right of the image. The barrels were being stacked up outside the pub that guarded the entrance to the tunnels. He had, of course, never intended to call in a bomb threat. How dare they try to imitate history.

William needed to see Jackson in person. The vote could not be derailed. He replied to Renault to keep watch.

Final calls from the atrium now as the session in the Commons was about to begin. Jackson would be heading there. William needed to snatch a few moments with him.

The Members couldn't get in the way.

30

ackson entered the House of Commons for the last time. At the end of everything, he would remember the total focus and attention he commanded. Everyone was in the palm of their Leader's hand. The same hand he had used to crush the loyal remains of his party. Without a Cabinet, Jackson claimed the front bench for himself. He glanced over to the other side of the Chamber. The opposition were threadbare, little more than twenty clumping together.

Backbenchers had their pick of the empty seats. The career politicians that were left drifted around. Motivation to network was draining away by the second. Jackson was left with the impression that this was a wake—yes, that was it, a Celebration of Life. The remaining MPs who survived his crusade against indecency turned out to mourn the loss of their temple.

The Speaker greeted him with the usual courtesy, the insincerity of pageantry. Normally averse to it, today he indulged it. They fiddled while Rome burned, but let them play one last tune. Jackson gave her a nod. It was time to begin.

'Honourable Members, we are gathered to debate a motion of no confidence in . . . this House. This is a serious matter of dire unprecedented constitutional scrutiny. I repeat, this government has no confidence in this House.' Rachel Jenkins spoke with a certain passion, wittering on for a number of minutes. After a few more details on proceedings, she finished and sat back, her smile morphing into pure concern.

Jackson rose and approached the despatch box. There was

no prepared speech this time, no carefully constructed diatribe from William. He looked around the Commons, his domain. Every moment he didn't speak, the weight of his unsaid words grew heavier. William couldn't touch him now. The future was his. He knew what he wanted to say.

'Britain was dying. I healed her.

   'Britain was under attack. I protected her.

   'The old ways have failed; this Chamber has failed.

   'Government after government have ignored the cracks, merely applying layer after layer of crusty cheap paint.

   'We have been preoccupied with points scoring, with the cycles of power, so much so that we never actually focused on making things better.

   'I blame myself; I blame all of us.

   'That is why it falls to me today to back this motion of No Confidence against Parliament and implore you all to vote to shatter this charade of politics once and for all.

   'Everything I have done, I have done for the country, and will continue to do so.

   'I am the last Prime Minister of Great Britain and Northern Ireland, you the last MPs. After today there will be just a Leader, with clarity of vision and a mandate of true purpose.

   'The House of Lords has already fallen, and do we miss it? Quite the opposite; we have passed policy quicker than ever. Less red tape, more common sense, people free to live their lives. If, as Sherlock Holmes said, the only true liberty is in death, then I will add that there should be liberty in life also.'

   Getting into his stride, the words flowed from him like the fastest river. The Chamber sat still in front of him; even the usual rustle of parliamentary papers disappeared. There would be no more printed, ever. He looked upon some of the faces, the same faces that had given him patronising advice at the start. They were leaning in now, looking for wisdom or solace in his words. Trying to discern their place in all of this. There wasn't one.

That first day, his maiden speech as Leader. Many stood, expected him to yield, wanting to table their own motions or grip the agenda. The fight had been beaten out of them. He was doing them a kindness now. Jackson gripped the despatch box tighter, readying the next sermon.

'We are putting the past out to pasture. I am here today not to—'

Someone stood up, out of the corner of his eye. Jackson craned his neck and frowned. It was that Phillips man—no, was it Peterson? It was probably the leader of the Opposition. Jackson didn't intend to yield. He ploughed on. Before he could get much further, a most unusual thing occurred. The standing Member spoke. Quickly and with a distinct panic tinging the words.

'Madam Speaker, it's now—we agreed, we have to do it now.'

Jackson whipped his head back to Rachel. She was sitting glumly. If her seat were sentient, she would have asked it to swallow her. She flicked her eyes from the standing Member to Jackson and back again.

'ORDER!' she screamed.

Jackson was dumbfounded. He just let it all play out. Rachel Jenkins was betraying him, trying to stick an oar in. She spoke again, this time standing, and shocked him.

'Our Leader will not be interrupted.'

Oh. This is new, he thought.

Jackson started to laugh, a large smile breaking out on his face.

'Thank you, Rachel.' Jackson turned to the standing Member and flapped a hand at him. 'You can sit back down now.'

That was the dying of the light; the brief disturbance was but a death rattle. Jackson, in truth, had expected more. He was planning to speak on, but what point was there now? The feeble attempts at stopping this were all played out. Jackson waved a hand back at the Speaker as he retreated from the despatch box. 'Rachel, do you know what? I think it's time we move straight to the vote.'

As he was sitting back down, a sharp scratching pierce screeched around the Chamber. An alarm was blaring, so loud that many covered their ears. Jackson's phone went into a fit with alert after alert.

He went for the phone as the alarm became interspersed with a robotic voice.

'Credible Bomb Threat—Please Evacuate—Follow Security Staff.'

Jackson had a security detail somewhere; no doubt they'd be pushing through the crowd imminently. Under normal circumstances they were banned from the Commons while it was sitting, but he had dismissed the plonker that controlled the security in the House early on. *Serjeant at Arms*, what a silly name.

A series of frantic messages lit up Jackson's phone like a tiny Christmas tree. He scanned. His contacts at GCHQ confirmed the credibility of the threat with CCTV footage. There was also a post on X from an anonymous account.

Parliament's Dissolution is not enough, it must disappear entirely.

Thirty-six Barrels underneath. Gunpowder, Treason & Pierce's Plot.

The alarm continued to tear through the Commons. It became hard to distinguish between the screech and the panicked shouts of the scurrying MPs. They couldn't leave; the vote was all that mattered. The Speaker's chair was already empty. Cowards, all of them.

'Sir, we need to get you out,' barked one of his security officers, grabbing at his arm.

Jackson pushed him away, his fury uncontrollable. 'You work for me. I want you to round all the MPs up outside. Find me a place to conclude this vote. That is all that matters, do you understand?'

'Sir, you are my responsibility—' The officer hesitated, caught between protocol and Jackson's order.

'Go!' Jackson roared.

The man hesitated for a second before rushing towards the fleeing MPs. As the mass of people surging out of the Commons turned right towards the exits, Jackson turned left. He broke off into a deserted side passage. It snaked around the atrium and reconnected back at the throng of people scampering away.

Ahead of him, just before a set of double doors that opened back into the masses, he saw movement. A dusty old wooden panel, the size of a small man, popped open and fell to the floor. A figure stepped out, grabbed it and pulled it back towards him. He was facing away from Jackson, but the man was undeniable. It was like Jackson was a teenager again, seeing this man stride out from behind the bus stop in Rotherham.

William.

Jackson studied him from afar. Even in the chaos, William was precise, composed. He hastily reattached the panel to the wall before disappearing on the other side. Jackson shook his head. It needed to be seen to be believed. Of course the old man had a secret tunnel.

The X post, the bomb threat, this was the Club's doing. Jackson was conflicted. Regardless of how they felt about each other, the vote to dissolve Parliament was in both their interests. Another of his security detail saw him and was now shouting for Jackson to follow him. Jackson was for a moment angry, before an idea hit him. He beckoned the guard over.

'Give me your gun.'

'Sir, I need you to follow—'

'Shut up, listen and give me your gun. It's that or I'll see to it that a law is passed specifically to make you . . . illegal.'

The man looked at Jackson like he was insane. Perhaps he was, but if so, he was now an insane man with a gun. Jackson waved him away, shouted about the importance of the vote again and continued walking toward the panel.

The old fart, in his hurry, had not reattached it flush. Jackson gave it a slight push and it sprang out again. He didn't think twice: Jackson slipped inside. There was a vestibule hidden back here. A second opening, bigger than the panel, lay directly ahead and sunk into the ground beneath Jackson. A great oak door lay ajar. He heaved it fully to the side and peered in. The air was damp and cold, the darkness barely broken by faint light spilling from somewhere further ahead.

William wasn't scared by the threat. He'd raced into this secret subterranean tunnel to confront the Club. Jackson wasn't afraid of the dark. He too would race in and confront William.

He stepped inside. It was almost pitch black.

William couldn't be that far ahead of him. The tunnels must snake, must turn and bend; where did they lead? After pulling out his phone and turning on the torch that barely penetrated the darkness, Jackson walked on.

Step by step, one foot in front of the other, Jackson followed in his father's footsteps down underneath Parliament.

THIS HOUSE

*Breaking News: Career alternatives for MPs — as experts suggest
Pierce will turn his attention to the monarchy next*

31

After navigating dusty old tunnels and weaving his way under Westminster, Mark came to the realisation that the Right Members Club had spent most of British history underneath Parliament, rather than in it.

Making it back from Parliament's post office, the other Members and Lucy were rolling the last barrel down into the open passageway. They were underneath a pub, an old forgotten place to drink near Parliament Square. The landlord left them to it—an understanding with the Club going back generations.

Each barrel had felt fragile, and the constant scuffing and bouncing into the narrow walls of the passageways meant that it was a challenge to keep the contents from spilling more than they had.

Zachary poked his head out of the opening. 'Are we sure about this?'

'I'm not sure about anything, mate. It's this or we just let William wash it all away uncontested,' Mark said. 'Besides, he just needs to know they're real.' He clapped his hands together, pulled out his phone and dialled. Horace picked up within two rings.

Mark wasted no time. 'We're set here. Give it twenty minutes after we hang up and then post it. Be specific.'

'All in hand, my boy—got it all written down.' Horace was calm and confident as he spoke. 'I'll be ready when you surface. In the meantime, I'll comb through the archive.'

Mark clicked off the call and opened up the *BBC Parliament* livestream. Notching the volume up, he heard the beginnings of the session. There was time while the Speaker directed the pleasantries and outlined the agenda, but with Jackson's new world of streamlined debate, it wouldn't last long.

At the bottom of the screen, a small green ticker showed the Pierce£ climbing, a bright, pulsing line edging ever upward as the time to the motion drew closer. The nation felt ready for change; Mark just didn't know what kind it would be yet.

Zach clapped a big hand on Mark's back. 'Ready to save the country?'

Mark nodded, and they filed into the tunnels. Within yards the livestream died, no signal, just torchlight and the dim glow of phones guiding them through damp stone. The air was cool, musty. As the noise of the pub faded, silence took over. They pressed on through twisting corridors lit by flickering torches, shadows bending with each step. Mark gripped Lucy's hand, half for comfort, half to stop himself turning back. The deeper they went, the clearer it became this wasn't one tidy passage to a single chamber, it was a maze, ancient and deliberate.

'Reckon William lit these?' Lucy asked.

'Maybe,' Mark said, glancing at the branching shadows ahead. The place seemed alive, as if Westminster itself was breathing around them.

'You're telling me that William has the run of this place?' Zachary said, his voice rising with disbelief. 'A massive secret network of tunnels right under the seat of power . . . the Club that's meant to be subtle and in the shadows literally has a labyrinth. How has this never been discovered?'

'Maybe they have—the Club lets them find a little bit. Like the passage in Parliament that was in the news,' Jessica said.

Susie followed up. 'William has engineered the impending fall of democracy. So bribing specialists and manipulating survey data must be a quiet afternoon for him.'

As they progressed down the narrow path, the gaps between the torches in the distance started to widen until they were no more. Mark rounded a dark corner and the five of them stepped through a low archway and into a lit cavernous room.

Susie was in awe. 'This place is huge. It must be the size of the Commons itself.'

It was at least twenty metres long, not quite as wide, and with a vast high curved ceiling that disappeared into darkness above. They found themselves at one of the corners of the Chamber. There were other archways and exits leading away from here. Mark felt weirdly reassured; it seemed that all paths eventually led here.

He ran a hand over the wall; it was smoother than the tunnels and far less damp. The Chamber's walls were divided into three bands like the rings of a tree: an outer layer of grey stone that continued across floor and ceiling, a middle band of matte black stone tracing the room, and ahead of him a faint green tinge rising into darkness towards the unseen ceiling.

Mark felt a nudge from Zachary and saw him direct a finger first along the wall and then to the centre of the room. Objects of some kind, silhouetted structures that danced as the light flickered, appeared to change shape with every chaotic movement of the lit torches.

'Benches.'

Lined up neatly on either side, at the start of the sparkling green segment of floor were beautifully carved benches. Reaching up as high as a couple of metres, they cast imposing shadows back towards the two men.

'Is this the Members' Chamber?' Jessica asked.

From their vantage point in the corner they could see through the gap between, and in the middle there was a flatter raised table. It was flanked on either side by two small platforms. Mark edged towards them, trying to get a better view, until a flood of recognition washed over him.

'It's the Commons,' Susie said.

'A replica,' Mark added.

They turned around and stared at him.

'Look at it—benches for either side, despatch boxes in the middle.' Mark pointed to the centre of the room. 'And look, that's a copy of the Speaker's woolysacky chair thing.'

'Christ, you eat your carrots, don't you?' Zach said.

'Don't know. Were they in Kevin's terrine?'

This must be the Members' Chamber, Mark thought. Barely mentioned in the archives, a secret even to the secret organisation. Mark reached up and ripped one of the lit torches off the wall. Its rusty clasp came away with only a modicum of effort. He wafted the torch above, revealing something. He stretched and stood on the tips of his toes, trying to thrust the torch away from him as far as he could.

'Look!' He tried to direct the gaze of the others above.

'What is that? Hold it still,' Lucy said.

'It's an engraving. Member for . . . Wrath. Mark, can you wave it over here, please.' Susie hurried over a bit further to the wall. 'Yes, yes, look! It's engravings of the Members' titles.'

'What on earth did the Club need this for?' Jessica asked.

Silhouetted by torchlight, the five of them stood stumped for an answer. A noise interrupted the blank they drew. It echoed around, as if the Chamber were now suddenly full of people chatting. It was a ghost-like sound that reverberated and seemed to dance with the torchlight.

'*Honourable Members, we are gathered to debate a motion of no confidence in . . . this House. This is a serious matter of dire unprecedented constitutional scrutiny. I repeat, this government has no confidence in this House.*'

'I recognise that voice.' Susie whipped her head around as if locating the source of the voice. 'Isn't that Rachel Jenkins?'

'The Speaker?' Jessica asked.

'There, listen!' Zachary was excited. Susie nodded and moved further along the wall until she was kneeling at an opening, a small rounded pocket in the stone, engraved with the word Envy above it. Mark waved the torch. It illuminated more pockets along the wall. Seven in total, each with a sin carved above it.

The debate in the Commons was echoing from each of them. Now they heard Jackson's voice from above. Susie tried to bend her head to see up the opening.

'Eavesdropping. I don't believe it,' she said with surprise.

'You mean this Chamber is directly connected to the Commons above?' Mark asked.

'It has to be. It's genius. Think about it: today we livestream *BBC Parliament* or wait for a text. But they couldn't back then. This is how they kept up to speed.' Susie was enjoying this.

'Maybe this was the first, but over the years they needed more ears, across the whole of Westminster. I bet there are loads of these rooms dotted around, connected with all these sub passages,' Jessica added.

The debate continued above; it was perfectly audible.

'Hang on. I think I've found . . . yep.' Susie said. There was a sound like a high-pitched scrape, as if two objects collided. It finished with a pop, and then once again they were left in silence. 'There was a disc lodged into the wall, like a spinning wheel,' she added.

'What did you do?' Lucy asked.

'Well, I spun it. I think it shuts the holes up, makes it silent. Maybe so the Members could chat freely. Sound carries both ways.'

Before they could fully grasp the idea, there was a new sound—steps, quieter at first but building in volume.

'Disgraces and degenerates. You found it alright, then. Wasn't beyond your primordial wits.'

Mark's skin crawled. He knew that voice. 'Renault.'

'Fallow.' Renault's smirk was unmistakable as he stepped into the light. A hideous shadow arced across the wall. 'By all means, call me Ren. Seems appropriate given all we've been through.'

No one spoke. They all watched as Renault dusted down his jacket with a performative calm. 'Already packing upstairs. They're demob happy. Parliament is going the way of Woolworths. Thought I'd take a souvenir.' He raised something in his hand, one of the ornate maces carried by Black Rod. 'Never know when I might need to knock some sense into a former backbencher.'

'A relic stealing a relic,' Jessica muttered.

'Speak up in the back. I've borrowed it. Democracy is on pause, so I think it will look nice on my mantel. What do you think?'

'You once told me about making jokes. Perhaps that was projection.' Mark rolled his eyes.

'Mouthy. You've come such a long way from that dreadful little office in Briarwood. William was clear, only the most useless, the most spastic of men. I couldn't believe my luck when I saw you. Let alone when you started talking. I texted him straight away. A whopper.'

Lucy tensed at that.

'Less of the speeches. What do you want?' Susie asked.

'Nothing. We all do nothing. Wait here for William. Out of sight, out of mind while we wrap up business above.'

'You're his lapdog.'

'His vision is flawless. It's the only logical way to ensure the future. Believe me, I've worked up close with politicians for too long. It only ever ends in tears. Tears of the cock for you, Fallow.'

'I'm only ever the punchline, I get it. William's coming, though, you say?' Mark shot a look at Zach and Jessica.

'Indeed. He knew you'd come. Try something to stop us. Afraid he had your number there. Your Club wasn't built on talent; no, it was predicated on the usefulness of uselessness.'

Zachary scoffed at that. 'Ren, Peugeot, Citroën. Whatever. If William actually inducted us but not you, then what does that say about your place in all this?'

'I'm nothing. I'm a facilitator for the end. You still don't get it. None of this matters—not the Club, not you, not me. It's about to be self-sustaining. All pleb inputs now. The Pierce£ is the mechanism. Every argument, every headline, every drop of outrage goes straight into the sentiment feed. And right now, it's about to skyrocket.'

'And then what?' Mark asked.

Renault tapped the mace on one of the stone benches. 'You're as slow as my bowels nowadays. Man alive. Once it reaches critical value, in enough wallets of enough of the public, then you can't stop it. You can't stop Jackson, I should say, that is unless you want to send the economy back to the Stone Age. The 2008 crash would look like a stroll round Harrods by comparison.'

He wasn't done; he stepped towards them and waved his mace straight at Mark.

'I've got an idea—an NFT of your crowning moment. The Fallow Incident immortalised for evermore. Can help pay for whatever scheme we launch next.'

Mark saw red, his calm cracking. He went to lunge but was blocked by Lucy.

His wife instead steamed forward, catching Renault by surprise. She kicked him square in the balls before planting a shiner of a left across his face.

'That's from both of us,' she said coldly, 'and in particular for that humiliating fucking news conference on our doorstep.'

Mark crouched beside Renault. 'One good thing, Ren, you've just confirmed our plan's working.'

Renault spat blood onto the floor and wheezed a laugh. 'You should run. This place will be your tomb.'

Mark looked at the man, then back to the others.

'We'll take our chances. Make Mr Fawkes proud.'

32

ackson heard them before he saw them. Muffled voices as the tunnel ahead blinked with light. His head pounded in the stale, thick air. He called out, his own voice echoing back.

'Hello? Who's that?'

A shape formed out of the gloom. Neither Renault nor William. But fucking Fallow and his goons.

'You?' Fallow asked, in shock.

'Me.'

Jackson felt terrible. He probably looked worse. The shoulders of his jacket were buffeted and snagged; his hair, always so immaculate, was now dishevelled. He tried to reassert himself. Standing fully upright, naturally unfurling into his 'Leader's Pose'. Chest out, stride wide, he looked to and from Fallow and the others.

It took a moment for the faces to click. Disgraced ghosts from William's briefings. Jessica, the mouthy redhead; Susie, the swot; Zachary, the pisshead; and Lucy, Fallow's long-suffering wife. The Right Members Club. He almost laughed. The country's political leftovers meeting with the hot plate under its foundations.

That wasn't all, though. Scraps aplenty. On the floor nursing a vicious black eye was the scourge of his premiership.

'Renault, hah!' Jackson chuckled. 'Good on whoever hit him. I think he had quite the queue forming.'

The benches drew his attention now. Looking up, Jackson

noticed the Chamber they were standing in. He took a few steps around, his head craned upwards.

'Jesus, am I imagining it or is this a carbon copy of the Commons?'

'Shouldn't you be upstairs?' Zachary asked.

Still looking up, he replied, 'It seems we have a bomb threat. I imagine that's your doing?'

Stony silence from them.

'No matter. I'll have you all arrested on charges of treason or terrorism, whatever works best,' Jackson said, still admiring the ceiling.

'Was that your big plan?' Fallow asked.

Jackson turned back to them with a smooth movement. His hand reached behind him and swiftly returned, brandishing a gun at Fallow.

'I usually have a script to follow, but recently I've learnt that I'm better on the fly. This is what I have so far.' He waggled the gun, directing them back to the passage.

'Heroic Leader foils copycat Guy Fawkes plot below Parliament and apprehends suspects. Whatever will the papers say when they find out it's you, Fallow? Motive's clear as day. Couldn't keep it in your pants, so you've flopped it all out under the Commons. Seedy, gross little man.'

'Well done, Pierce, you've caught me red-handed again.' Fallow couldn't resist.

Jackson smirked. 'Like a select committee here. All that's missing is the cameras.'

'Knowing your dad, no wonder you're this fucked up,' Jessica shot back.

Jackson laughed it off. 'You can't choose your family, can you? Don't worry, I'll make sure you get your fifteen minutes of fame. The more disgraced MPs the better. Fuel to the fire.'

'But you still need William,' Fallow said. 'We're just the grunts. The bomb threat bought us time, that's all. You'll just reschedule the vote, or William will. He's always lurking. What will Daddy say when he finds out you've got your hands dirty?'

'I don't need him anymore. The country is mine. Right now, let's get a move on. I was hoping to have this all wrapped up in time for tea.'

Then came the sound. Not echoes, more footsteps. Slow, deliberate, the kind that carried authority even through stone. Each one closer, sharper, until the Chamber itself seemed to hold its breath.

'This is a nice little gathering, isn't it? The final debate, if you like.'

It was William. He emerged from an opening recessed below the copy of the Speaker's seat. Jackson recognised the threat, and shifted the gun in his hands.

William noticed Renault and laughed. 'Well done for keeping them here, old boy. Gave you a bit of trouble, I see.'

Jackson was being ignored. 'William, this ends now. We need to get the vote back on.'

'There he is—the boy wonder himself. I didn't even notice you there,' William said with a certain glee. 'Yes, yes, in time. But first we need to make sure this particular loose end is tied up. Let's have a seat, shall we?' He gestured over to the benches. 'We can resolve this amicably. It's all rather messy right now.'

Jackson led them to the benches. He took up position by the Prime Minister's despatch box, while Fallow and the rest shuffled to the opposite side. Renault limped to the Opposition bench when William beckoned. The debate was forming. Almost.

He adjusted his stance, the gun steady in his hand. Politicians were told never to point, but he wasn't really one of them. He aimed where he pleased. For the first time all night, he felt something close to control.

'Right, let's make this simple for everyone,' William began, his voice carrying over the stone like an echo of the Commons above.

Jackson resented how easy, commanding and too natural his father's voice sounded. It made him feel like a boy again.

Then came a crash. Jessica, the redhead, tripped over one of the pews, her phone clattering across the floor, the sharp crack of the screen bursting slicing through the silence.

Jackson almost flinched. William just laughed.

'Careful, old girl.'

'Get on with it. What do you want?' she snapped, picking herself up.

Before answering, William wandered closer to Jackson, planting a torch in the arm of the Speaker's chair like he owned the place.

'That's better, hands free. Right, what do I want? That was the question. Well, firstly, Jackson, put that bleeding gun down. You're fooling no one.'

'Don't tell me what to do, old man.'

'No, of course not. That's never worked out for you, has it?'

'I don't need you anymore. The country is mine.'

'Son, you're—'

'Don't call me that.'

The word crawled under his skin. His grip on the pistol tightened until his fingers ached. He told himself he was still in control, but William's tone was shifting the ground beneath him. Every syllable felt like William was writing his lines for him again.

'We're on the cusp of everything we've wanted,' William said, his voice dripping with disdain.

'You've wanted, you mean,' Jackson bit back.

'Oh, come off it. You've not loved every single second of playing Prime Minister?'

'I'm not playing. I am the country's Leader.'

William's face twisted. 'You believe it, don't you? You think you're here to make Britain a better place. There is no making Britain a better place. There's only purging it. Making it pay for what it did to our family. To Linda. Your mother.'

Her name hurt him. Jackson's stomach flipped. He'd not known her, not really, but that name still had power from all those years ago. He had only sealed it behind his podium smile and photo ops. Now it was loose again, bleeding into the air.

Renault grimaced and turned to William. 'I told you, he was getting carried away.'

'That you did.'

'I'm standing right here. Look at me,' Jackson hissed. The gun shook in his hand.

William sneered. 'And what would I see? A sobbing teenager? A lonely orphan? I gave you a future, an opportunity. I made you everything you are. Not the state, not the system. Me. I even picked your name. You're too belligerent to realise the significance of it, aren't you?'

'It's just a name,' Jackson said, but even to himself it sounded weak.

'Born from the death of the Union Jack, Jackson,' William continued, voice quieter now. Drawing people in. 'Linda Purcell. Purcell, from Percival, from Pierce of the Vale. I thought it poetic. Jackson Pierce.'

The words hollowed him. His father's silly, obnoxious games embarrassed him, reduced him to tenuous wordplay. He could feel the certainty draining from his body. His name wasn't even his. Nothing was. He wasn't the man in control of a nation. Everything he had done, every step that he had tried to run away from William's grasp, had only brought him closer to this moment.

Jackson was a ventriloquist's dummy that thought himself to be the puppeteer.

'You used me,' Jackson whispered.

'Speak up, Leader. No,' William said, delighting in the cruelty. 'I made you. Every speech, every policy, every photo opportunity, mine. Jackson Pierce, your legacy, my game. And now . . . checkmate.'

Something in Jackson cracked. The gun trembled; his hand was slick with sweat. The world around him, the torches, the benches, the faces, started to pulse with the rhythm of his heartbeat. This wasn't power. His life was a sham.

'Give me one good reason not to shoot you right now!' Jackson screamed.

'Emotion. You're weak. I spent a long time building a dam inside you, to stop this useless, needless lip-quivering. But it's burst. You're drowning in the past as the mission slips away.'

Jackson felt fifteen again. As he regressed, his fingers loosened on the gun. When he finally spoke, it wasn't the Prime Minister talking at all. It was Tommy Purcell.

'I didn't need a mission,' he said, voice breaking. 'I needed a father.'

William laughed. 'A father? You're weaker than I thought. I should've left you in that children's home in Rotherham.'

And just like that, he'd been knocked out of slipstream. The airs and graces of power dispersed like rain in the wind. The gun grew heavier in his hand, and all that remained of his composure slid away. He'd come down here to prove he was in control, but William was still holding the strings.

More than that, the man who'd made him was unmaking him.

33

Mark's gambit had been simple on paper. Hell, it was a letter, after all. But it's in those gaps that chaos can thrive. Get William and Jackson together and let the truth eat itself alive. If the confrontation barrelled its way towards mutually assured destruction then the Members would need to be ready to seize their moment and wrestle back control of the nation.

Jackson looked finished. It was this thought, obsessive in Mark's mind, that encouraged him to stand up and give his maiden remarks in Parliament. Sort of.

'The Right Member for Wrath, William, you talk very well. Indeed, the dismantling of your own son is very impressive. But ultimately without Renault and us Members, you're nothing. Sorry, I should keep it political while down here.'

Mark waved his hands as he stood up on the benches to make his point. 'I mean to say, the Dishonourable and quite Right Members do all your dirty work. Renault is the Alastair Campbell to your Blair; that probably makes Jackson, Prescott or Brown, and someone has to be Blunkett, don't they? But don't worry about that for now.'

A laugh from Jessica and Zach as Susie and Lucy pulled faces.

William's eyes narrowed. 'Very good, and what would you know about politics? You were an MP for a week, if I recall. Out of all the sorry cases on that bench, you are comfortably the worst of the lot. A disgrace to them, a disgrace to the country and a disgrace to your wife.'

Mark didn't flinch. 'So was it Renault who dispatched Esther Murphy for you? Or another faceless lackey?'

'Christ, so you created your own catalyst? Congratulations; conspiracy theorists will run riot with that for generations,' Lucy added, cottoning on to Mark's play.

'It changes nothing.' William addressed Jackson. 'Forget these losers. Get back up there and reschedule the motion. I'll hold them here.'

Susie joined in now, seeing a pattern. 'It all makes sense. William only hires useless disgraces, doesn't he? He told us as much. The Right Members Club is a home for dysfunctional, broken things to waste their time running errands for a bitter old man. It stands to reason Renault and Jackson would be the ideal candidates.'

'Good point, Suse,' Zach agreed.

'In summary, he's a cowardly little shit stain. I yield.' Mark bowed as he finished, to the roar of approval from his own supporters.

That was it, the straw that broke William's back. He yelled for silence, lunging forward in anger towards the benches. Towards Mark. He was a big man and as he moved, his shoulder knocked the torch that was embedded in the stone despatch box. It loosened.

A second from being clobbered by the same fist that had put Derek down, Jackson pointed his gun to the ceiling and fired.

A flash of light pulsed, and a burning acrid smell lingered. Jackson demanded calm. As he did, there was a staggering moment. Almost symbolic, Mark thought. Tiny little flames burst into life, running haphazardly towards the many arch-ways that led out of the Chamber. Small flames, sparks of dancing orange, winding around, lighting the pathways out. It must've been the fluid. It sloshed and leaked from the barrels as they were loaded into the tunnels. The whole place ran downhill, so it snaked all the way to the Chamber, leaving streams back up and out.

Jackson now turned the gun towards William.

'You stole my whole life!' Jackson roared. 'I went along with murder, with hurting people. For you!'

William went to move towards him, but Jackson was having none of it. He fired a warning shot, just missing William. With a *thwack* it took a chunk of stone off the opposition's despatch box.

'Behave, boy. I'm trying to help you to rule the country,' William snarled.

'You've never helped me; you've only ever helped yourself.'

Jackson had zeroed in, lost his peripherals, as from behind, a beaten and sore Renault hit him firmly in the back. His knees weakened and as he doubled over, the gun was wrestled away from him. Renault promptly delivered it to the smirking William.

The little trails of fire began to smoke now, more light, more illumination, everyone cast in changing shadows.

William now levelled the gun at Jackson, 'Go over there with all the naughty children.'

Jackson bumbled over to the benches.

'You've made this hard, ever so hard for me. I would have let you all live, perhaps. Let the vote pass, end Parliament and then we could all rest.'

'Would that really be the end, William?' Jessica asked him, pain in her voice.

'That depends on the people. Most live their lives just trying to get enough stuff, enough money, enough material wealth so they can stick their fingers in their ears and ignore the rest. I think they'd do just fine without all of this.' William gestured above.

'But people rely on the government,' Jessica came back at him.

'They rely on the state,' William said firmly.

'Is there a difference?' Jessica asked.

'If we let the vote pass, we'd find out. But alas, here we are. You've given me plan B, this little light show on the floor. Your barrels, I presume, Fallow?'

'Embalming fluid. Bacon lube. I'm assured that whilst flammable, it's not explosive. Just needed to get you all hot under the collar to come down here. I didn't want to be the guy who blew up Parliament. Sorry, William, no get-out-of-jail-free card here.'

'Clever,' William said. He turned to Jackson, raising the gun. 'I guess I'll have some use for you yet, son of mine. We'll get that vote rescheduled, and then we can talk about your departure. I've a few waiting in the wings to take stewardship of Britain—a new path forward.'

'You've lost it,' Lucy muttered.

'Not at all,' William said, pacing. 'The Pierce£ will carry us through. Happy people don't ask questions. Keep calm and carry on, a singular goal for the nation to serve. They'll keep sentiment high, keep the algorithm fed, and the country will run itself.'

'Is that even how crypto works?' Susie asked.

'The tech people assure me it is,' William snapped. 'And if it's not, they'll invent something else. People don't need leadership anymore, they just need a concept. Something to believe in. Jackson gave me the idea with that ridiculous social voting. Perhaps the future doesn't need a face after all.'

'You're fucking insane, William,' Lucy said.

'And you're a wife to a wanker; what would you know?' William barked, swinging the gun towards her.

Mark reached out, resting a hand on her leg. He'd throw himself in front of her if he had to.

'Here's what happens next,' William said coldly. 'We kill Lucy and Mark. The others are optional, depending on how they behave. And then we frame it so the Prime Minister's loyal advisor saves the day.' He nodded towards Renault. 'How's that, Ren? A spin doctor as a hero for once.'

Mark felt the sweat run down his face. William was deadly serious; Derek's death proved that. There was no bluff left in him. Even if Mark took the first bullet, William would keep firing until he got what he wanted. He looked at Lucy, managing the faintest smile. They had failed. And now they would die here.

Through the depressed silence Mark thought he heard a new noise, from his right, in one of the passageways. He was imagining it; it was an echo of something. But then Zach turned his head. So did Susie and Jessica. They both smiled at Mark as if they'd just won the lottery.

'What is that?' William heard it too.

'Do you not know what this place was for?' Susie smirked.

William snarled at her. 'I know everything about the Club, silly girl. It's just a joke, like the Omni, a pathetic joke about the Club's disdain for tradition.'

'We thought so too, but the devil is always in the details, isn't it?' Susie said.

'It's the little things, William.' Jessica smiled.

'Explain. Cut the crap.'

'Eavesdropping.'

Susie took over. 'Little air vents that run from down here up to the Commons. It's where the Club would come to get intel on what was going on in Parliament. Highly impractical, but it did the job.'

'We heard the opening of the debate earlier. We also learned that sound travels two ways. Earlier, when I slipped, it gave

Susie the cover to open the seals back up,' Jessica said with a smile.

'Shame we don't get signal down here,' Susie said.

'I do.' William said, his mind half elsewhere. 'I made sure of it.'

'In that case, boss, could you open up the livestream for *BBC Parliament*?' Susie instructed.

William looked perplexed, his eyes going from Susie and Jessica back to the sides of the Chamber, the noises getting louder. He kept the gun pointed at them while fishing his phone out of his pocket. A few taps and there it was.

He turned the phone around. It was just the empty evacuated Commons.

'Turn it up,' Jessica coaxed him.

'Turn it up,' echoed back through the phone.

'SHIT!' Zachary yelled.

Sure enough, about ten seconds later, a rather loud '*SHIT!*' screeched back through the phone.

Mark cocked his head. He couldn't believe it, the whole event, this final debate—argument, scuffle; everything below Parliament broadcast in near real time to the world.

The noise from the passageway reached a crescendo; muffled voices and footsteps bounced out of the archway. There were people; lights blared back at the benches, dazzling them. Mark heard shouting from the corner they'd entered from earlier.

'I reckon that will be the police, William—oh, and maybe some press. Want to make a statement?' Lucy laughed at him.

William screamed in defiance. The gun was raised again. It was pointed at Lucy. His finger closed around the trigger. Mark jumped to protect his wife, leaping crossways to cover her.

As he sailed past, he hit his head hard on the stone of the benches.

The bullet never came; even in his dazed state he was sure of it.

From out of nowhere Jackson had vaulted himself up and smacked into his father. Jackson was determined, full of strength. He grunted and groaned before winding back and clocking William with a full-on headbutt. William dropped the gun, and it skidded towards Mark on the floor.

Jackson looked at him. A cold demand came. 'Fallow, give me that gun, now.'

Mark refused. He hated William, but he wanted justice, not revenge.

He wasn't going to choose to help Jackson kill him.

'You don't need to do this, Jackson.'

'It's the only thing I need to do.' The reply was as certain as anything ever said.

Jackson picked up the gun with a controlled grace.

Mark was powerless. Everyone screamed. He could swear he heard the police yelling for calm. Lucy dived down towards Mark as time slowed down.

Renault made for William but hesitated just a second too long.

A shot—a single shot. It rang through the Chamber like Big Ben.

William reached towards his heart. There was a smoking hole that began to redden. A deep crimson colour seeped down his shirt. He fell backwards and was silent.

Jackson dropped the gun and returned to the backbenches.

Parliament was in recess.

WRATH AND RENEWAL

Breaking News: A Promise Broken? The Rise & Fall of Jackson Pierce

34

It's often said that a week is a long time in politics. In that case, the three weeks since the shocking events beneath Parliament must feel like a lifetime. So much remains unclear. Perhaps we'll never know the full, bloodied truth of that day.

Jackson Pierce's resignation was almost inevitable after his broadcast confession was heard around the world. Coupled with the violent confrontation that led to the death of a man claiming to be his father, Pierce's position became untenable.

This marks the end of a movement that began with tragedy: the death of Esther Murphy, now confirmed to have been a covered-up murder.

As more details come to light, authorities have confirmed the arrest of Renault, the Prime Minister's Special Advisor, whose real name has been revealed as Lenny Groves—a former politician who reinvented himself as a detective within the West Yorkshire Constabulary.

What began as quiet suspicion has spiralled into the exposure of a double life. Police sources say Groves' involvement runs deep, and it's now expected he'll spend the rest of his life behind bars.

The Pierce Promise started with a lie. A lie that spiralled into chaos, propelling Pierce into power and leaving a nation divided in its wake.

While the police investigation into Pierce remains confidential, the debate rages on publicly. Some see Jackson as a saviour, the brave Leader of a new Britain prepared to act. Others paint Pierce as the greatest liar this country has ever known, a demagogue for the ages, a man who would jeopardise the public's health and safety for political gain. Who knows if there will ever be a consensus? Who knows if that's even his real name?

What we do know, however, is that the nation today will take its first step in moving on.

That is why I join you live, here at a polling station for his former seat of Lambeth Central as the country looks to elect the first cohort of MPs since Pierce's Premiership, with one of the candidates sure to raise an eyebrow . . .'

'Not one mention of the Club. Horace really did come through, then?' Lucy's question distracted Mark from the television.

It was a bright sunny Thursday around lunchtime; the light poured into their living room. Mark and Lucy relaxed on the sofa, Chunk curled in between.

'Bit of a masterclass, for sure.' Mark took a sip of his tea as he nodded his head.

She grabbed Mark's leg. 'How did he manage it?'

'Reading. Lots and lots of reading. William was a bit of a bragger, loved to write lots down in hard copy. After Horace sent the bomb threat post, he got to work. Sifting through years and years of files and documents. With decades worth of his own financial records too, after he'd cross-referenced everything, he had the list of contacts that William leant on.'

'Forensic accounting. A man after my own heart.' Lucy smiled.

Mark gave Chunk a stroke. 'Yeah, a *who's who* of ghosts, spooks, coppers and civil servants—all in William's pocket.'

'And they just agreed to help Horace out and cover all this up?' Lucy asked.

'Yes and no. Turns out these rather smart people all felt quite dumb when Horace explained what William was really up to. Acute embarrassment from aiding high treason is a hell of a motivator.' Mark took another sip and frowned. 'Besides, we're not covering it up. Jackson lost everything and now must atone for what he did, and the country gets to move on. We're just editing ourselves out.'

'Not Renault, though. Man, what a creep,' Lucy said.

'William wrote everything Renault did down. An insurance policy if he ever needed to *deal* with him, I guess. We just pointed the police to it. Open and shut, I believe is the term,' Mark added.

Lucy's face turned serious for a second. 'I don't know if I'm okay with just writing William out of it all. He deserves to be hated.'

'He'd want to be hated if it meant his ideas were remembered. This way is better; we forget about him. The country never knows; one side never has a villain, the other a martyr.'

Lucy scrunched her face. She'd need more convincing, but she let it slide for now. 'What next for Jackson? Have you decided?'

'Up to them. I've made my case.' Mark got up and kissed Lucy before ruffling Chunk on the way out. 'Big day today, though. Focus is all on you! Avoid dogs. And webcams. I've got to get going, or I'll be late. See you later.'

The Omnibar was quiet when Mark arrived that afternoon. A far cry from that night three weeks ago . . .

The immediate aftermath of William's death was hectic, to say the least. Renault had tried to use the chaos to escape, but Zach had put him down with a staggering punch. Out for the count, they had left him for the police.

It was Jessica who had snapped everyone else back to action. She led them all, including Jackson, to one of the passages. They escaped just in time, as the police and media found their way down underneath Parliament, following the smoky signals wafting up from the embalming fluid fire.

Mark grabbed Jackson, forced him to come with them. 'He saved Lucy's life,' Mark proclaimed once back at the Omni, the group filling the Fawkes Tavern as if it were a Friday night out.

Jackson sat alone at one of the tables as the others cast glances and pointed fingers at him. The silent defendant in a trial, he sat motionless with a fixed stare into the middle distance.

Zach started on the other side of the debate. 'He's a liar and a murderer, and a populist idiot to boot. He's responsible for all of this.' His emotion carried convincingly for a few of the others.

It was hard to recall exactly who supported what and when as the Members got stuck into the debrief back at the Omni. It was the type of debate where there were no wrong answers and it was possible to flip-flop entirely reasonably multiple times.

As a stalemate was reached, a lull in the back and forth allowed Mark to put an idea forward.

'It's not Jackson who did this. He was a puppet. A puppet to the man that almost broke us too.'

Immediately, it softened some of their stances on him. The empathy spawned from knowing what it felt like to be controlled by William.

'It would be the easy choice to lock him up and throw away the key. But just because it's easy, does it mean it's the right choice? He's been a victim of William since—what, since he was fifteen?'

'What are you suggesting, Mark?' Zach looked perplexed. The others stood there in silence, waiting for whatever was to come next. Mark felt something build in him. He looked at Jackson and he didn't see evil; he saw a fool, sure, someone who had made many mistakes. But someone who deserved a chance to put it right.

The next time Mark spoke, he addressed Jackson directly.

'Your dad, our boss, he did all of this. Yes, you fell for it and you helped him, but so did we. You were never in control, and neither were we. Look, Jackson, it's up to you. Do you want us to leave you to your fate, or do you want a chance to do better than William?'

For the first time since William's death, Jackson engaged.

'Just a chance . . . that's all I want.'

Today the Members weren't in the Fawkes Tavern. Mark found them cosy in the corner of the 1920s bar—renamed the Strong Bar in honour of Derek.

Horace had pulled at the Club's purse strings and made sure his family members were looked after. It was the least they could do.

The Members were deep in discussion, so Mark poured himself a pint and wandered over.

'So here we are.' Mark was a little bit nervous at what sort of response was coming. He had offered a cooling-off period for his idea, letting the dust settle on the emotion of that night.

Horace stroked his chin. 'It's been three weeks.' His pause increased the tension Mark felt in his gut. 'I was unsure at first but I think it's worked.'

'Yes, me too,' Jessica said.

'We need to move on from hate. From anger,' Susie added.

'Alright, *Yoda*,' Zachary said.

Mark looked at him, his head was down. He slowly raised it. The tiniest smirk was forming in the corner of his mouth.

'Look, I was dead against it. But time heals. It makes sense, I guess. Sure, let's do it . . . boss.' Zach winked at him.

Mark spat out some of his beer. It dribbled down his chin and onto his trousers as he furiously looked for a napkin. 'Boss?'

Zach replied, 'The Right Members Club needs a leader, and I can't think of anyone—'

Mark cut him off without meaning to. 'I thought we were doing an *everyone's equal* thing, and besides, it would be Jessica, surely?'

Jessica smiled at Mark. 'I don't want that gig. Much happier just helping out. I can be your second-in-command if you like. But be warned, I had my fingers burnt before, so will keep you honest.'

'Mark, the Club is about disavowing self-interest. I can't think of any better example than how you've acted. You got us through this; you've been the voice of reason in a time of crisis.' Susie placed a hand on Mark's shoulder.

'So go and get your first inductee, Leader,' Horace said with a wink.

Mark was stunned. He got up and walked away while his head processed the conversation. He could barely dress himself in the mornings and now this. His legs wobbled a little as he traversed the Omni. He steadied himself and knocked briskly on the door.

A fresh-looking Jackson Pierce, his hair shorter and sporting some glasses, opened it. There was a slight resemblance to William, but it wasn't overly strong.

'Mr Pierce, Jackson, if you'd like to join us in the Strong Bar.'

'Which one is that? I've been here three weeks and I'm still confused.'

'I just follow the noise.'

The two men shared a laugh before a different look fell over Jackson's face.

'Look, Mark, you've gone to bat for me. You didn't need to, the things I've done to you and the pain I've caused.'

'I thought about that for a long time. You're right, it hurts. But it was my fault, my choices; those were my actions. I take responsibility for them, and as long as you can do the same for yours, then we have no problems.' Mark smiled at him before adding, 'You are not your father, or at least, you don't have to be.'

'Jackson Pierce was my father's invention. Can you call me Tommy? Tommy Purcell.'

It made sense to Mark. It clearly meant a lot to Tommy.

'I've got a lot of work to do, but I'll do what I can to restore the title Member for Wrath to its former glory,' Tommy said.

'Glad to hear it.'

He wasn't wrong, there was a lot to do, and the afternoon passed in a blur. While Jackson Pierce's government was over and his motion of No Confidence against the Commons dismissed, his tenure had left a mark on the country.

The interim coalition government, formed by all major parties, aimed to prevent another *'Pierce Moment'* where a cult of personality derailed the nation's politics. A new group of MPs even championed blind voting, prioritising policies over politicians to safeguard against such manipulation. The House of Lords was dissolved, and in the month since, policy was passed quicker than ever. Some lauded this as progress, while others pointed to the disasters it enabled: the Workforce Growth Bill that disrupted lives like Ana and Seb's, and the Fast-Track Food Production Scheme that gave rise to 'Zombie Bacon.' These laws lacked scrutiny but were also quickly rectified under the new 'One House' system, proving its potential utility.

The Pierce£ cryptocurrency and blockchain were dismantled and placed on the scrap heap. That wasn't without its challenges. Young Dean worked around the clock to put the lid back on that particular can of worms. No one could say, still, how it all really worked.

Modernisation wasn't completely off the table, though. But it did come with a debate now: not all tradition is bad, nor is all efficiency good. Britain needed to weigh each aspect pragmatically, rejecting ideas clung to for tradition's sake while ensuring reforms served the people.

The renewed fire for political debate ran parallel to the one that had roared for days beneath Parliament, a physical reminder of the damage the Pierce Promise had left behind. Thirty-six barrels of burning fluid proved a challenge to stop. The blaze destabilised the House of Commons, allowing it to sink, destroyed, into the Members' Chamber beneath. It left the new coalition with a rare opportunity: to rebuild not just Parliament's literal foundation but its purpose.

For the Right Members Club, the duty was clear. It needed to change, no longer blindly maintaining the status quo but holding politics to a higher standard. It would now serve as a safeguard to the people. Politics needed to evolve, not to chase hollow efficiency or cling to outdated norms but to create a system worthy of the people it represented.

Mark walked as fast as he could once off the tube in Lambeth. He was absolutely drained of energy from his day at the Omni, but he didn't care. He had somewhere to be and someone to be there for. As he arrived outside the fancy-looking building, he found himself indulging in a sense of irony.

He was doing it. It wasn't as an MP, and none of it was official, but Mark was working to make everything a bit better.

His worst fear used to be that one of his lurid intrusive thoughts would come true. That one of the horrific scenarios his mind acted out for him would become reality, and then one day, it did. But without that, without the humiliation and pain that came, he wouldn't have learned what was truly important. He discovered that if you only ever lived in fear of what might happen, you'd miss the point of living at all.

He could be who he wanted to be despite it. It was his choice; he was in control—always.

Lucy stood waiting, her face set with quiet excitement. Mark walked over, a huge smile spreading all over his face.

'Here we are! How's it feel?' Mark asked, nodding towards the stage, where the returning officer was fiddling with the microphone.

'Waiting for the moment to be over,' Lucy replied, her nerves evident from her wobbling hand.

He'd been a part of this journey before with Lucy supporting him. But tonight, this was all down to her brilliance.

The returning officer stepped up to the microphone. The room fell silent as she began to read out the results. Mark's heart raced as the official tallied the votes, his gaze darting between Lucy and the stage. It was close, but in the end, she did it.

'. . . therefore, Lucy Fallow is returned as the Member for the Coalition Party for Lambeth Central.'

Lucy cried. Mark embraced her, his chest swelling with a pride he didn't think possible.

She was shaking with surprise and happiness as she approached the microphone and began to speak. Mark beamed at her.

'I never thought I wanted to get into politics. Never thought it applied to me. I was wrong. It took a horrible wake-up call to shake me into the real world. Two of my closest friends almost had everything stripped away because of the actions of the last government. Too many of us paid too little attention for too long. Thankfully that crisis has been averted, but how many more will suffer silently, invisible to us all? I have a lot of learning to do, and I won't always get it right, but I promise you, Lambeth Central, that I will do everything I can to try and make your lives better.'

Lucy spoke from the heart, and by the time they got home later that night and managed to fold some mediocre pizza—not delivered by Scott—into their faces, they were ready for bed.

The pair were by themselves, without a constitutional or mental health crisis, for what felt like the first time in a century. A new dawn was breaking, and Mark and Lucy would be there for each other to make sure it was a clear, bright sunny day.

They kissed, as if for the first time, before Mark's leg kicked the pizza boxes across the floor, causing Chunk to fly up the armchair in a panic.

With sauce sinking into the carpet, Mark got up to get some kitchen roll. It was then that his phone buzzed. He glanced at it. It was a text from Jessica.

Sloth?

There was a link to a news story. Mark laughed and swivelled his phone round to Lucy.

MP admits to posting nuclear codes on X.

'How do you embroider a card?' Mark said.

'The Right Members Club will be back to full strength,' Lucy replied.

Perhaps. In truth, it was Mark and Lucy Fallow who were.

AFTERWORD

The Right Members Club will return

ABOUT THE AUTHOR

Louis Urbanowski finds writing about Louis Urbanowski in the third person creepy, so will stop.

I gave up a twelve-year career in software sales to follow a dream. You are now reading it!

The Right Members Club is my debut, but not the last book in this world. Thanks to my wonderful wife, I had the courage to start a brand new career.

Writing the story of Mark Fallow felt cathartic. My OCD is a constant, rude writing partner. This book is for anyone who thinks everything feels a little too mad nowadays.

You can follow my writing at UrbWrites.Substack.com.

Thank you for buying my silly little book!